Reaper's Report

VANA DESCHENES

iUniverse LLC
Bloomington

REAPER'S REPORT

iUniverse books may be ordered through booksellers or by contacting:

iUniverse
1663 Liberty Drive
Bloomington, IN 47403
www.iuniverse.com
1-800-Authors (1-800-288-4677)

Because of the dynamic nature of the Internet, any web addresses or links contained in this book may have changed since publication and may no longer be valid. The views expressed in this work are solely those of the author and do not necessarily reflect the views of the publisher, and the publisher hereby disclaims any responsibility for them.

Any people depicted in stock imagery provided by Thinkstock are models, and such images are being used for illustrative purposes only. Certain stock imagery © Thinkstock.

ISBN: 978-1-4917-0829-3 (sc)
ISBN: 978-1-4917-0830-9 (e)

Library of Congress Control Number: 2013916858

Printed in the United States of America.

iUniverse rev. date: 10/4/2013

Contents

Prologue

I'VE HAD THIS JOB SINCE 1915. GOT IT AFTER A HAND grenade blew me into the other world. I literally was resting in peace—no, in pieces. It's okay, just a little reaper humor, folks. When you have been dead for close to one hundred years, it is not so hard to reflect on one's own demise. Besides, I do this for a living now. I am the Reaper! Nice to meet you. How do you see me? With a fancy title, a black robe, complete with a farm instrument that no one knows the name of? Yes, we got rid of that thing—yes, the thing, the word that is on the tip of your tongue. I'll wait. I have all of eternity. The scythe! It is a type of sickle. Yes, that is no longer part of the standard uniform. In fact, the robe itself is no longer part of the uniform. One other thing that may surprise you is that I am one of many. There is not just one reaper. The world is too big with seven billion people running around on it. And dying is an occurrence that happens every second. One guy cannot handle all that.

We reapers are pretty low on the corporate ladder. Even though we are the first thing people see when they die, we do not have a lot of clout in the corporation. Oh yes, death is a business like everything else. There is a whole corporation devoted to it. Like most corporations, we had some restructuring, a change in corporate culture and a makeover. We changed with the new millennium; we became a lean, mean machine. More about the corporate structure later, but before I lose you, let me give you a brief history of how I became the Reaper.

Where was I? Oh yes—*bam!* Blown up! So the guys upstairs, they were short staffed. They didn't really expect such a casualty rate in the Great War, as it was called at the time. History would later change the name to World War I. With all the people who died in it, the corporation was woefully unprepared. There were guys dropping off right, left, and center, not just because of the war, but because of diseases, the flu, and the occasional STD complication. The reapers who were working, were fed up, overworked, overstressed, and not properly compensated. They demanded that more people be brought on staff.

So there I was in some field in France, not even a fancy field like Vimy Ridge or Flanders—you know, one of those spots that made the history books. I was just in a field, adjacent to some mortared farmhouse in some little French town.

That morning, I had a croissant, was ordered back onto the lines by my sergeant, and some guy offed me with a grenade a few hours later. That was that. So when a ragged, tired old guy showed up after the big explosion, I was quite confused. He, on the other hand, was efficient and in a hurry. This was the notification I got:

"Okay, corporal, here it is. You have been blown up. See over there? That is what used to be you, so you're dead now! You have some options available. You can take your chances with Peter at the Gates, but he is very picky about who he offers admission to; it is kind of a VIP deal now. Purgatory is always open, but it takes awhile to get the hang of things in there, and you never know when you will get out. Or I can give you a job here, collecting souls, and you can see some of your buddies and family. Plus, there is a pretty comprehensive pension plan and some administrative perks. Interested?"

So that was how I was offered a job delaying the afterlife and enjoying the worldly delights once in a while. It was better than the alternative, so I signed up.

My first job really affected my overall job performance. It took me six hours to convince a trench soldier that he had succumbed to mustard gas and that no, he had not put on the gas mask correctly. I had to explain to him what happened, and by the time he finally understood, six hours had gone by. During that time, I had other fallen men just wandering around, freaking out about seeing their bodies on the ground—or, in the case of one guy, in a tree. They were wondering what had happened and turned to each other for answers—answers that they did not have—so that led to only more mass confusion and panic. That was a sticky situation for me, and I learned I had to get better at my job. While the guys upstairs wanted a familiar face among my fallen soldiers, they also had a schedule to keep and a quota to fill. Eventually I got the hang of it. I had become more like my reaper and was quick to the point and efficient. The men who I would escort would usually be greeted with, "Yeah, you're dead now. No, that bullet really gotcha. Yeah, it is not so bad here ... No, I have not brought your grandma here to greet you. She's upstairs. I am more of a middleman. Don't worry; your girlfriend is about to be hit with a bout of yellow fever, so you will know someone soon." That kind of speech.

Over the years, I have gotten better still and have found a middle ground between quick and impersonal and compassionate. I now follow a schedule and try to read people in order to break the news to them in the best way and get them onto the next level as soon as possible. I have worked for ninety-nine years, and although I do not have a glorious employment record, I have managed to do all right. I have met some interesting people, seen the world, and realized that, all in all, it is not such a bad job.

That brings me to the corporation I work for. "Deaco" is short for Death Corporation. It has been around since, well, since people started dying, so quite a while. It works the same way as many corporations, with several departments and business units. There is a hierarchy of employees, managers, and big shots. The objective of the, shall we call it company, is to streamline the process of crossing over from the world of the living to the afterlife. With the massive expansion in population on earth, the company has grown, and there has been an ever-growing demand for reapers. There has also been an expansion in development of the paradise properties and even dream consultants for those nouveaubodies who do not know what they want to do with their afterlife. The company itself is pretty standard, and just like any company, they have accounting, public relations, and marketing departments. We make the employee joke that "only human relations is different."

Each of us reapers has a certain quota of persons to help through this adjustment period. Once completed, we can retire. Retirement is in the Gated Community with our own little version of paradise. Peter is the security guard there, and he has held the position for as long as anyone can remember. One tip: when you meet Peter, do not call him Pete! He hates that. He makes sure your paperwork is in order and then points you to your own piece of paradise.

Once there, many fulfill a dream that they never lived on earth. Some become big movie stars living in penthouses. Some become millionaires living on golf courses. Others have more humble visions of paradise wherein they surround themselves with friends and family and have infinite picnics. For me, it is a cabin on the lake with plenty of fish that are always biting. I have picked out my spot on Lake Fish-a-Plenty. I currently visit it while on vacation. I have to pay my dues as a reaper in order to own it outright, so I work. Good news is I have almost acquired it. Today will be my last day.

The thing most people wonder about is how I look. Well, to put it bluntly, unremarkable. I would blend into any crowd. I am not a skeleton, I am not dressed in a robe, and I am in no way intimidating. Most people, when I approach them at the end of their lives, are incredibly unimpressed with me. They inform me immediately that I was not what they were expecting. In most instances, they expect one of two scenarios—either a scary reaper to lead them into the abyss, or a loved one to help them through the transition. In reality, their loved ones are busy enjoying their own paradise. Half the time, they cannot be bothered to come out to the initiation into this new way of being. It is akin to asking a relative to pick you up at the airport. They wonder why you cannot take a cab. Are you not an adult wearing your big-boy pants? To get there is a pain. There is traffic, and the parking is expensive, and they had plans for that particular time when you need them to come get you. So come on your own, because for them, it is a hassle. Your loved ones are glad to entertain you once you make your way there. But it is like the holidays; you go over to their house, they see you, they like you for a few days, and then they want you to leave. They have their own thing going, and you have to do something in your own afterlife.

Deaco, like I mentioned, has been around for a while. Its best-performing business unit is the Disasters Department, founded during the plague. At any given time, this department institutes huge events in order to increase the level of intake for Deaco. The department has business units for regions it is responsible for, and those are divided by the six continents: Africa, Asia, Australia, Europe, North America, and South America. (Antarctica does not have its own department on account of no people living there.) These business units orchestrate major disasters. For instance, today we got a memo that they are working on a bank holdup at corporate headquarters. The memo was entitled "Thousands of suits in one building, and the potential for massive casualties." The Disasters Department loves to use the term "massive casualties." In fact, the department's slogan is "Spectacular disasters—massive casualties."

Besides man-made catastrophes, they also do natural disasters. Volcano eruptions, major earthquakes, tsunamis—you name it, they've had it. This department has the most funding and the biggest special effects. It takes a lot of effort and planning to execute one of these disasters. Really, it is about seizing the right opportunity. There is always a human who can make a mistake, and when that mistake happens, you bet that Disasters will take advantage of it.

Take for instance the *Titanic*. The captain goes way too fast, and the guy in the watchtower is drowsy and cold. He spots the iceberg too late and—*bam!* The ship collides with the iceberg and goes under a few hours later. It was a great opportunity for Disasters to up their quota.

Same goes for Chernobyl. Here was this country, part of the Iron Curtain entrusted with nuclear power. They get excited; it is a big opportunity. This can power a bunch of factories and houses and make life better. They are chosen to harvest this power. Sure, but Gregor gets a little tipsy and does not insulate a reactor properly. You had better believe when Nora, a junior account specialist, learned of that, she saw her big opportunity to create a disaster. After the disaster, she got promoted for showing initiative.

The Chile earthquake, well that was created by Diego, and in a surprise that people are still talking about to this day, he let the miners live! There was this nail-biting situation where they were trapped for days and days, and the world watched, at first thinking they were goners! Then, as there were still signs of life from the mines, the people of the world were holding their breath, hoping that the miners would survive. All over the world, people came together to pray and hope that these poor, unfortunate miners would come out alive. And they did! Man alive, the excitement from people all over the world when that happened. Unbelievable! The miners went on every TV show possible and maybe even on *Oprah* (I don't recall; I don't get cable up here). So everyone was happy. Except, of course, the Disasters Department who thought that things would end differently.

Diego had some explaining to do. He managed to spin it as a public relations triumph that made our whole company look good. He said it was collective prayer, the coming together of all people. Goodwill, the power of faith, and the triumph of the human spirit made the survivor miracle happen. He said that humans needed a "miracle," and they saw it; they saw mercy from harm and death. He said that this was what Deaco had accomplished by letting the miners live. And that it was what it needed. Because when you are a company in charge of killing people, well, sometimes you need a little good PR.

Truth was Diego figured out that one of the miners was his great-grandson. And to be honest, he did not want him to meet his maker. Instead, he wanted him to go home and live a happy life with his family. So Diego put his own ambitions aside and halted the disaster. When you start a disaster, to stop it, man, there is a lot of red tape and bureaucracy in order for that to happen. That is why it took a few days for them to get out.

See, initially, to start a disaster, it is a pretty expedited process. One sees an opportunity and puts in a request to management to run the scenario and orchestrate the event. Management looks over the feasibility of the situation and evaluates the potential gains. In this case, the amount of casualties the situation would cause. Like any department, Disasters has a quota they need to fill annually. Since disasters by nature take a lot of people, only a few are needed each year to fill the quota. Management looks at the potential number of people who would be harmed and also the originality of the disaster. Management loves out-of-the-box thinking like a cruise ship sinking, the meltdown of a nuclear reactor (sidebar: that was the first of its kind in originality, as the technology was not available before). And Nora, the one-time junior account specialist, quickly found herself promoted to behind a management desk because of her creativity.

Management does not like monotonous disasters. That is why there aren't volcanoes erupting all over the place all the time. Volcanoes are destructive and efficient, but if they happened every, year they would become boring. Instead, used sparingly, they are one of nature's most spectacular disasters. The only exception to overusing an event is the guys managing the Midwest; they seem to throw in a tornado every year to meet their quota. These guys have been in that position for centuries, so everyone looks the other way until they retire.

So when a request for a large-scale disaster gets approved, something is changed by the powers that be (the Adjusters) on earth so that a perfectly normal situation goes horribly wrong. And then the catastrophic event happens.

Reversing this is a big, complicated process and hardly ever occurs.

In North America, there is a disaster at a multinational bank. Therein is a hostage situation. At Deaco, the building is abuzz with chatter and speculation on the outcome. The excitement in the air is palpable; this is going to be exciting.

Deaco has their own camera crews that record big events so that all staff members can watch the events unfold. You can also tune in to the human television stations to watch the reactions. Yet Deaco TV is pretty reliable in showing the preparation for the event, the behind-the-scenes action, and they get the best footage.

People at Deaco are looking at their screens, watching the action unfold. They watched as the masked men sneaked through the emergency exits and climbed the stairs to the various floors of the bank's headquarters. They watched as the robbers got into position. Then they entered and did the standard guns blazing, telling everyone not to move and that they were there for the money shtick.

This particular situation was handed over to Karl to manage. Karl is what would commonly be referred to as a douche! Big house, big ego, reasonably sure small penis. He runs a situation in a way that makes everyone around him feel small. They do all the work, and he gets all the credit. I should know. I am one of the peons he knocked over in the game.

Karl and I started together in Daily Deaths (the department I work in). Remember how I mentioned that in the Great War soldiers were dropping like flies? Yet there were not enough reapers to assist with collection. I died and was offered the job of a reaper with a retirement package that would allow for my own version of paradise upon conclusion of service. Well, that is how Karl got his start too. It was just that Karl and I fought on opposite sides. We laughed about it, how we died fighting each other only to work together in death. We even hung out after work. He was a fun guy; he was single when he died and was always up for a good time. He dragged me out whenever I was having a tough day.

We talked about the crazy things that were changing in the world. We shared thoughts and ideas. I told him that I thought planes were fascinating. Whenever one flew over the trenches in the war, it took my breath away. It was too bad (at the time) they could only transport one to two people. "But make no mistake, they are going to be the way people travel in the future! They will go great distances and will allow people to see the world faster than any ship can," I had said.

"This blimp that everyone is talking about being the perfect mode of transportation seems more like a death trap!"

At the time, I found it strange that he got a gleam in his eyes but dropped the subject. A few days later, he was promoted and working out of Disasters Department. He was in charge of a little event you may have heard of: Hindenburg! He totally took my idea and ran with it. He never gave me any credit. Even when I brought it up, he laughed it off in a condescending way. He said, "You're not jealous of my big idea, buddy, are you? Had you thought of it, you bet I would have shared the credit. Heck, both of us would have run the event and would be working in Disasters now. It is not nice to be petty when someone has a good thing happen to him!"

Then he started rumors stating I was jealous of him and was acting up. He told anyone who asked him about me that he felt sorry for me because I envied his success. He wished it was not the case because we were friends and came up into the reaper service together.

Well, that was when Karl ceased to be my friend and instead became a constant pain in the neck. He walks around with a big smile and a cavalier attitude, thinking he is on top of the world.

I am no Karl, he gets all the cushy jobs. Gail, my manager, started out with the *Titanic*. She was a suffragette back in the day and insisted on being able to do the job just as well as a man, so here she is now managing a whole lot of them. Initially, they gave her a heart attack on the vessel, but then some guy had to speed up the boat, another guy didn't see the giant iceberg, and—*bam*—she gets over fifteen hundred (1,517 to be exact) souls on her first job. She stayed in Disasters for a few decades and then requested to go to Daily Deaths. She says she prefers to work on individual cases rather than orchestrate events that cause massive casualties.

I haven't had anything big, ever! I missed my opportunity with Hindenburg and then never thought of something interesting enough to submit to Disasters. Since today was my last day, I didn't really expect anything big to come my way.

It was going to be the usual workday. Now the standard is about one hour allotment to each "new arrival" or nouveaubody. Yes, reapers have had to change the language as well with the times. Okay, moving on. We have regular days. Ours are just a bit longer, with twelve-hour shifts in human time. So let's say a guy dies at 3:36 p.m. We won't get another person until after 4:00 p.m. What we do in between that time is up to us as long as we get the person to processing before moving on to our next person.

We meet in the morning and are given our list of "new arrivals" or nouveaubodies that we are responsible for collecting and getting to the transition port where they are taken for processing. That department takes care of them for grieving, counseling, and arranging for the afterlife. This has reduced the backlog on our workflow. We used to have to do all that, but now we just have to get them on earth and bring them back to headquarters. We have, in essence, become glorified delivery boys.

As it so happens with time, people forget about you. In the end, they are not really interested in your story. I am interested in stories. The lives people lead, the way they end up, and the people they leave behind. I began writing each story down. Twelve stories a day, 365 days a year. That is 4,380 stories of people's lives in one year. I have been doing this for close to one hundred years. That is 438,000 souls, give or take a few, that I have encountered in my time at this job.

This was my last Friday of a typical workweek. People were getting ready for the weekend. It was the end of August. Some were squeezing in their last vacations before getting the kids back to school, and others were enjoying sleeping in. Some were slaving away at the office. Today was my last Friday at work ever, so I walked through the office and took my usual seat at my desk. The phone's red light was flashing, letting me know I had three messages. I picked up the receiver, entered in my password, and they began to play.

Message one: "You have won an all-inclusive getaway on Paradise Cruises—" Deleted. Stupid telemarketers! You can't get away from them, even here!

Message two: "Hey there, ho there, how there, how is your day shaking up?" Message paused.

It was from Karl. I debated listening to the end of it out of sheer curiosity to see what he wanted. But on second thought, I realized I wouldn't have to deal with him anymore, so who cares what he wants! Deleted!

Message three: "We are confirming your arrival at Fish-a-Plenty Lakeside Cabins tomorrow. Your cabin has been prepared according to your specifications. Please call back to confirm your arrival."

Now that was a happy message. My own piece of paradise ready and waiting for me. I allowed myself a few minutes of daydreaming before turning to the task at hand. The people I would be paying a visit to today.

My list was already waiting for me in a sealed envelope. I opened it and took a look.

Kevin Johnson	Daniel Smith
Emmie Guggliatti	James Stamford
Duncan Crabapple	Chang Wong
Nancy Grace	Luke Kozlovski
Steve Brown	Joe Tanner
Elsie White	Lacey Lowe

Gail came into our section wearing her crisp suit, and she cleared her throat before she made the announcement.

"Well, everyone, I am here to assign the quotas for the next two weeks. Usually we do this on Mondays, but today is a special day, as one of our team is retiring." I heard the creak of chairs as my coworkers turned in my direction. Suddenly it felt like a hundred eyeballs were looking at me. I squirmed in my seat and felt my face turning red. I looked up at the crowd, and all eyes were on me. One pair of blue eyes caught my attention, Deborah's from Accounting. Our eyes met, and she waved. Deborah was looking mighty good.

Gail smiled and continued. "Well, seems like everyone knows who that is. So as he ends his career, I wish to say on behalf of everyone, thank you for your great job! On behalf of Deaco, I am here to present to you this golden scythe!" She whispered in my ear, "It is plated with 18-karat gold." She handed me the scythe statue, a few camera flashes went off, and the crowd applauded. And Karl got up—fricken Karl, he really annoys me with his whole golden-boy routine. Of course he would get up when there was applause. I almost wanted to tell him to sit down, that it was not for him, but he spoke up.

"If it is all right, Gail, I would like to say a few words." After she nodded, he continued. "We started at about the same time. Remember that you were blown up and I was shot? I always felt you were like a brother to me! You always had a way with people, the personal touch with your clients. I usually have to deal with a lot of them per hour, being in the Major Disasters Division, but I envied you for being able to have the workload that lets you have a slow kind of day. Yet throughout your whole career, I know you wanted to have a hectic, big event. So ... I know we usually don't do this, but I was assigned a hostage crisis that will develop today, and I want you to have it, buddy!"

And before I knew it, Karl was strolling over to me with a big grin on his face and gave me a hug. I didn't know whether to recoil or reevaluate my judgment of the man. Kind of hard to do because I had spent decades thinking of him as a pompous, arrogant, boastful ass. Either way, I finally had a cool assignment, so this was going to be a good day to end my career. I felt the expectant eyes on me, so I said, "Thanks, everyone, for your support. I had a good career, and I am pretty happy. See you tonight at my retirement party, but for now let's get to work."

Chapter One: 1:00 p.m.

DOWNTOWN ON A FRIDAY IN THE FINAL WEEKS OF SUMMER is when everyone who is working wishes they weren't. Around 1:00 p.m. is when you see those who took a long lunch pretending to rush back to work, when in all reality they were thinking about their weekend plans and how to slack off for the next four hours. Others come down with a fake illness like stomach pains. Or they use the excuse, "It's feeling like a cold is coming on. I better go and not get anyone sick." Then as soon as they clear the building, the work clothes come off, and weekend partying begins. It is a pretty routine experience for Fridays in the summer, especially when that summer is coming to a close.

Today would be a little different. A big event would impact many in the city. In most instances when people are not affected on a large scale, they usually go about their day oblivious to the crisis around them. A guy could have a heart attack, and someone on another floor of the same building would not know about it. He or she would only learn about it come Monday, when it is gossip for a day. Then that person would not be brought up again, as topics that are more interesting, like *American Idol*, come up. It is interesting how tragedies in general do not affect a large amount of people. Of course, that is unless there is a jumper in front of the commuter train that delays traffic. People feel it then. When they speak about it, usually it is not a comment like, "That poor man. How awful was his life to have to end it in such a tragic and violent way?" Instead, most people say things like, "How insensitive of that jackass. Now he has to ruin everyone's day by jumping on the tracks. Why couldn't he stay at home and hang himself like a normal person?"

Well, today was going to be a day when a lot of people would be inconvenienced. It would be a situation that would leave a lot of people talking, and more than for just a day or two. There was going to be a hostage situation in the middle of the business district. And here is how it unfolded.

The armed men had already entered the Credit Bank headquarters and had taken control of the flagship branch. This flagship branch was located on the first floor of the corporate headquarters. In the hustle and bustle of the holdup, one of the employees pressed the silent alarm button to notify authorities. It was what the manual told them to do, as well as place a dye pack if possible and comply with the demands of the robbers. Usually robbers would try to get as much money as they could and exit the building as quickly as possible. Rather than just take the money and run, these robbers had stayed behind, lingering and tying up hostages. There was a general concern in the branch, not just for the safety of the employees and customers, but also wondering what the men had planned. Why did they not take the money and flee when they had the opportunity? Why instead were they lingering in the bank as if waiting for something? What those being held hostage inside the branch were unaware of was that they were a diversion, and that there was a bigger plan. At this time, there were masked gunmen holding up not just the branch, but every floor of the tower. Men had positioned themselves and were holding everyone hostage—everyone from the administrators to the executives, right up to the CEO. One of the executives had managed to send a text to his golfing buddy, the police commissioner. "Being held hostage, whole building under siege. 911. Send help!"

That was how the police commissioner found out. From there, he contacted SWAT and the captain of the downtown precinct. The captain's secretary alerted the guy she was dating, Chip Rodgers, a local news reporter. He too got the message by text and read it after covering a human interest story of a particularly fat cat being rescued from a tree. When he read it, he knew that he had a scoop on his hands and that he had to act immediately in order to get coverage. He used his earpiece to communicate with the studio and demanded to speak with the news director. Todd, the news director, asked, "What's going on, Chip?"

"We have a hostage situation downtown, confirmed by my source at the police department. I want to go down and cover it. I don't think anyone else has caught wind of this yet."

Now Todd had been in the business for fifteen years and had not come upon a hostage situation, and he knew a hot story when he heard it! A hostage situation in the middle of the day was bold and brazen and, most importantly, filmable in time for the six o'clock news! "Get down there!" was the order given to Chip.

Todd explained the situation to the anchors doing the twelve o'clock news and told them that they may run past the hour slot in order to give Chip an introduction, and he could lead off with the story as soon as he got there. Once the anchors heard about it, their eyes lit up. This was an actual story with multiple segments that would bring in lots of viewership. This was the kind of story that they dreamed about covering when they were studying to be broadcast journalists.

Their eyes were sparkling, their hearts were beating wildly in their chests, they were excited, but of course in the interest of professionalism and decorum, they had to adjust their attitude and adopt an informative, formal tone to report on this crisis.

The news came through the earpiece that Chip was in position. The female anchor looked at the camera in all earnestness, used her concerned voice, and stated, "We have just received news of a hostage situation occurring at Credit Bank. Our news camera is there to cover this event. Chip Rodgers from the Channel 5 News team reporting."

The senior anchor took over and stated, "Hour one: Chip Rodgers joins us now from the scene of the hostage situation. It is reported that masked persons have entered the bank and have taken hostages."

Chip Rodgers said, "I am here on the corner of Main Street and First Avenue where Credit Bank corporate offices are located. We have very little information on what is occurring inside the bank. All we know now is that the silent alarm was tripped inside the flagship branch located on the first floor of Credit Bank. Police have been called to the scene and will respond to the situation. Unidentified sources claim there are hostages inside the building. Tune in to Channel 5 News, as I will be here reporting on the events as they unfold."

Nurse Willow ignored the report in the background playing in the waiting room of the hospital ward where she worked. She did not much care for Chip Rodgers and pretty much tuned out whenever he spoke. He could be reporting that a missile was aimed directly at her house, and she needed to get out. He could look directly into the camera and state, "Nurse Willow, the trajectory of the missile is aimed at your home. You need to get in your car and drive off to save your life. You only have a minute to do so!" And she would change the channel with disdain for the man and ignore whatever he said. So she was oblivious to the situation that had begun to transpire a few blocks away from her.

Willow walked into the small room located on the west wing of Mercy Hospital. It housed three people per room. Unfortunately, these were small sick patients. It was always a bad sign when a patient was moved from one of these rooms into a single room. It meant that they had taken a turn for the worse. What was even sadder was that Willow was in the children's ward.

Kevin Johnson, a boy of seven, was diagnosed with leukemia and was likely not going to go home this time around. Willow had a soft spot for Kevin, a brave boy who had gone through six treatments already. He had a sister, Merry, like Christmas, born five years earlier in the maternity ward on Christmas Eve. She had bright pink cheeks covered with freckles, blue eyes, and auburn hair. Kevin had sandy curls and the greenest eyes she had ever seen. Nurse Willow thought that he would have been a heartbreaker if he had the chance to grow up. She often came in to talk to Kevin, and he would tell her about the fort they were building in his room and the progress of his train collection. Merry was there too, usually eating Kevin's Jell-O because it wiggled like the Blob in her favorite cartoon movie. Kevin and Merry were very close. Both their parents were workaholics, but they did have a wonderful nanny, Consuela, who brought in baked goods (that Kevin could hardly keep down because of his illness), and she told him wonderful stories, of fairies, superheroes, and angels. They kept him company during visiting hours. Willow often liked to take her breaks with Kevin, during which they colored a picture in his coloring book and talked about anything but his illness. Willow suspected Kevin had a bit of a crush on her and thought that was very sweet.

Today he looked tired and a little paler than usual. Even though he was not feeling well, Kevin made sure to pay her a compliment. "You look really pretty today, Willow!" Willow thanked him for the compliment and stated that he made her day better, like only he seemed to be able to do. She was glad to have him be the best part of her day. At this, the little boy blushed and heroically said to Willow, "I am really enjoying our dalliance!"

Dalliance? thought Willow. She was not even sure what that meant. She made a mental note to Google it as soon as she was out of his room. She thanked him for the compliment and she said she was likewise enjoying the dalliance. She stroked his hair and promised to be back to check on him later, but that he should get some rest. If he got a nap in, she would bring him a cookie when he woke up.

Once she was in the corridor, she slipped out her smartphone and typed in "dalliance" and learned it was a brief love affair. She thought, *Oh God, I just told a little boy that I was enjoying it.* She would have to correct that soon.

Sadly, when it came to her love life, it was not at all promising. Her personal life was a mess. She had always unwittingly attracted the bad boys. She never pursued them. It was just that they always seemed to find her. She tried dating all kinds of men—short, tall, skinny, fat. Yet they always turned out to be players, law breakers, addicts, and in one very special occasion, hiding his career as an adult entertainer and high-end escort. Him, she brought home to meet the parents. It led to a very awkward conversation a few weeks later when her dad had to explain where he had seen Tom before. It was one of those movies he would have otherwise never admitted to owning. *Sexy Lawyers and Naughty Law Breakers.* Willow was unaware of Tom's career and sadly had never seen one of his performances on screen or in person. In the most awkward conversation she would ever have, her dad assured her that on screen he looked like he could show a lady a good time, but he was not the type of man he could see settling down with his little girl, especially to start a family with, for he figured when the grandkids had to bring their parents in for career day, well, the whole situation could get kind of embarrassing.

So there she was, pretty and nice and successful in her job and single. She blamed the city she lived in; globally it was known for having beautiful women and some of the worst guys on the planet. Yet she held out hope of one day meeting a good guy, and she had recently started to see someone. She worried about being duped by guys who seemed to be a good catch—only to find out how bad they really were. This time she decided to skip the steps of falling for a guy only to be disappointed. This time she decided to judge the book by the cover go out with a bad boy and at least know what she was dealing with. It was refreshing really. Here he was, this new man, the classic bad-boy type on a Harley. He had rugged good looks, tattoos, and a six-pack. She just hoped that in their city he wasn't involved in some sort of criminal activity. Joe Tanner—that just didn't sound like a criminal. Besides, he went to the gym near her house, and criminals didn't go to the gym. It was where she met him, at a yoga class, and yoga classes were not the type of places guys went to pick up girls.

She did a quick round around her ward, checking in on her patients. She finished by checking in on Kevin. Kevin was asleep. He looked pale, his lunch was untouched, and his vitals looked incredibly low. Willow made a mental note to check in on him a little bit more that day. She was looking at this cute little guy and vaguely heard the story that was blaring on the television. When she turned to face the screen, she saw the face of Chip Rodgers and immediately turned the TV off.

Ah yes, Chip Rodgers. She had made the mistake of falling for his pretty-boy face and local celebrity status one night at the bar down the street from the hospital. She had had a particularly rough day, and he bought her a drink. In turn, she commented on his coverage of factory shutdown that left a lot of people out of work. They commiserated that night, and she ended up taking him home. In the middle of the night, she woke up to hear rustling and see the moon shining on Chip's butt cheeks as he was searching for his pants in the dark. She turned on the lamp on her nightstand and asked, "What are you doing?"

He exclaimed, "Oh, found them!" grabbed his pants, and proceeded to pull them on. Then he said the words every girl dreads hearing after a rash hookup. "This was fun!" She knew it was the kiss of death, the words the guy uttered to a girl who he didn't find particularly challenging and who he was definitely not interested in seeing again.

Willow made the classic desperate mistake of asking, "When will I see you again?"

Chip replied, "Any time you turn on your television to Channel 5 News, darling. I am sorry. I just really am very busy with my career and can't make this a regular thing. I'll call ya." He never did. She cringed at the memory and bolted out of the room, looking for something to preoccupy her mind instead.

After a few minutes of charting and a few more minutes of filing, she went up to the maternity ward to grab a quick coffee with her friend Amber. Maternity always had chocolate lying around from some mom who got chocolates with nuts and the mom was allergic to nuts. Both Amber and Willow enjoyed nuts, so they made a grab for the chocolate. It was a good place to have a coffee, some leftover chocolate, and a few minutes of fun conversation. This time, Amber told her about a woman who had delivered with her water membranes intact! That is an extremely rare occurrence, like textbook rare. Usually they burst, and that is when the very expectant mother states, "My water broke," and is rushed to the hospital. With this mom, hers had remained intact. And Amber, being an overexcited type of girl, decided to exclaim that very fact! "Oh my God, they are intact! I have never seen one of these! This only happens in textbooks! Crazy! Man, the other nurses are going to be jealous they missed this!" Which led to the mom wondering what the heck was happening and if everything was okay. The doctor gave her a dirty look and asked her to go get gauze. Okay, gauze was not even needed, but she was sent out of the room in a somewhat tactful way. That same doctor was not so tactful later when he talked to her about not freaking out the patients.

Amber's retelling of that story definitely got Willow's mind off her dating life and even what was happening with some of her patients. Once her coffee break was over, she headed back down to her floor.

Willow being on the floor with Kevin and on the maternity floor with Amber stirred a memory for me. The thing about hospitals is that they are a place of life and death. Most people perceive them as a place of healing. I have wandered the corridors of many hospitals in my time, and for my profession, it is a place of death. But for me personally, it is a place of life. I have seen babies born, people with diseases cured, and health restored.

One of the babies I saw was Kevin Johnson. It was a few years back. I was on a mission to collect an elderly man who was a war vet. Frank was his name. He was adventurous and spry in his younger days. As happens with age though, he became a shell of his former self. His skin was covered with age spots, and it hung off his bones in wrinkled bundles. He needed help walking, and his sight was clouded. When I entered the room, he saw me as one of his brothers-in-arms. It was easy to carry on conversation, as I had been to war myself and both of us had served in France. He fought in the Second World War, and I in the first.

He started with stories about how he spent his free time when he was not engaged in battle. Apparently he had an amorous affair with an Emilie, a resistance fighter. She had joined a band of rebels against the Vichy occupation. This was when France was occupied for a few years.

He met her in a bakery. She was sipping a coffee. He was trying to convey in his poor French which pastry he wanted to the baker behind the counter. It involved much pointing as he tried to show the baker which confection he wanted, and the baker selecting every single item around it but the one he wanted. Seeing him struggling, in perfect English she asked, "Do you need assistance?" He turned and saw an angelic face framed with dark blonde curls. She was wearing one of those little French hats that were en vogue back then, with a little black cardigan over a white blouse and a dark gray skirt. She took his breath away. He could not speak, and all he could manage was a series of quick nods, which in hindsight he thought made him look rather foolish.

She stood up from the table and walked over to the counter and said, "*Le patisserie avec le cochon et formage s'il vous plait* (the ham and cheese pastry). *Deux!*" Two? He understood that one. He knew how to count to ten, say please and thank you, and ask for the toilet. She had ordered two pastries. She looked at him and said, "Well, since I helped you, I figured this can serve as a thank-you." And she took a big bite. What struck Frank was that she looked demure, but she was feisty. He knew then that he wanted to get to know her better. So they went for a stroll. She talked about her childhood growing up in Alsace-Lorraine, a border province between France and Germany. Her father had fought in the first war and came back with stories. She was raised to be a fighter and to be vigilant should France ever be occupied again. She didn't tell him about being a resistance fighter until much later, but they carried on a romance while he was stationed there. He fell madly in love and proposed. Asked her to go back home with him. She broke his heart when she said that her true love was her country and she would never leave it. So she declined his proposal and left him in disarray.

The other GIs watched him mope on the boat home for weeks. At first they teased him about love lost to French girls and saying, "Join the club. We've all been dumped by an Amalie or Claudette." But as the days turned to weeks, they realized that he was really in love and very much heartbroken. So they eased off teasing him. When he returned home, he looked up his high school girlfriend. She had not married, so he proposed on the first day they were reunited. She had carried a torch for him all the time he was overseas, so she happily accepted. They went on to be married for fifty-six years.

When he finished that tale, he said to me, "Come now. Before we go, I want to show you something." We took the elevator up to the third floor, the maternity ward.

The nurse there greeted Frank with a smile and said, "Back again for another visit, huh? Can't stay away? Have fun!"

Frank walked me over to the area where the little babies lay. He pointed to one with a little white cap and blue blanket and said, "See there, that is my great-grandson, Kevin. My first great-grandson. Now how lucky am I to have lived to see that?" I smiled and acknowledged that indeed he was a lucky man. We stood there for a bit looking at Kevin. When Frank got physically tired, we walked back to his room, he lay down to sleep, and a few minutes later he passed.

That one memory stood out to me—when he took me to the maternity ward, the place where life begins. Most people assume that anywhere I go, anything I touch dies. It is not the case. One only goes when it is their time. I can be surrounded by people, and they won't drop dead like flies. But not many know that. Like I said, most expect that I carry death with me, and they shy away from bringing me near anyone else for fear they will meet with that deadly fate. So it was unusual when Frank brought me to see his great-grandson, Kevin. A new baby, and he showed him off with pride. I saw, smelled, and touched new life. Today I was there to take that life away. It made me wonder if the paranoia people have about me carrying death was true.

Willow had been out of Kevin's room for an hour when she heard the bustle of doctors rushing to his room. She knew that the worst had happened and that the disease had finally taken its toll on the little guy. She knew that he would not come back, but she had gotten so attached to this wonderful little boy that with tears swelling up in her eyes, she began praying for a miracle.

It was while she was praying that I walked into the room to see Kevin lying on the bed. As the Reaper, I have a job to do—guide people from the word of the living to the afterlife. Okay, collect them and bring them to processing, but that does not sound nearly as interesting. As one dies, the body is left behind, and the spirit or soul, however one chooses to define it, leaves the physical body and looks for a place to go. That is where I come in, to help with the confusing transition. I let them know what has happened and guide them to Processing. Processing lets them know where they need to go. They fill out the nouveaubody paperwork and walk them through the next stages. From there, a team of experts takes care of each client. There are client services and support if there are any questions. A concierge to assist in tasks, etc. Servants to take care of your needs. There really is a pretty good setup for each of the NBs.

The question I often get asked is "Where do the bad people go?" Well, the really bad ones, like the mass murderers, etc., I cannot talk about, as it is classified. But your average run-of-the-mill bad guy who is disliked by most people he meets ... well, remember how I mentioned concierge and servants? Ta da! There they are. Man, there is nothing like seeing a Wall Street scammer having to be the butler to an average barber. They hate it! It really is kind of like a personal hell for them. If they complain or are rude, they get transferred to an even more difficult client. Also, it is physically impossible to harm anyone in the afterworld, so management is never worried about these guys getting out of hand and clubbing someone. Eventually, when they learn their lesson, start enjoying serving others, and become better people, they get to have a paradise of their own. Although to be honest, I have heard of some guys who never learned their lesson and became mannies to septuplets. They are literally in doo doo all their existence.

I cut short my daydreaming and returned to the task at hand. Collecting Kevin. I made a sweep over the body, and suddenly little Kevin's essence came to life. I began the speech.

"All right, Kevin, welcome to the other side. I hate to break this to you, kid, but you died today. That is the bad news. Good news is that you were really well behaved throughout life, and you have a tree house filled with toys, and your Grandpa Thomas is there. He is there with his dad, Frank, and he looks forward to seeing you again."

He responded, "Wait no, not today. I mean, I know I am sick, but not today. I gotta give Merry her birthday present. I hid it in the house before I left last time. And I want to say good-bye to my parents. Can I go back, just for today? Okay, you can come get me at the end of the day. I promise I will come with you, but I just wanna see my kid sister and parents, 'kay?"

The kid looked so desperate and cute that I actually considered doing it. I had never broken protocol in nearly a century on the job, and I had seen some cute kids. But then again, it was my last day on the job. I could collect him at the end of the day.

"Okay listen, kid, I am really breaking protocol here, I mean breaking the rules."

"I know the word protocol. My mom's a lawyer; she uses it a lot."

Smart kid. I thought about it and said, "Right, so I have to follow rules, but I will make an exception. You know the word exception, right?" He nodded. "Okay, so I will make you a deal. I will come and visit you at the end of the day, and by then you should say good-bye to your family. The only thing you can't do is tell anybody about me, okay? That is the deal!"

He strolled up to me with his little pinkie out and laced it around mine and said, "Deal. End of the day, I will be ready, and I won't say anything to my family."

I was very skeptical. It was my last day on a ninety-nine-year-old job, and for the first time ever I had made an exception and granted an extension to a seven-year-old boy. I hoped I would not regret it.

Chapter Two: 2:00 p.m.

"Well, hot damn, we've got ourselves a situation here!" said Chip to his camera operator. "You think I can get one of them daytime Emmys for covering this story?" The camera operator began to reply but was quickly cut off by Chip.

"I am sure I am gonna win something for this, big ol' hostage situation in the middle of the day. Brazen reporting by yours truly. Oh yeah, they are gonna give me some kind of shiny news reporter award for this! Hey, makeup girl, come over here with some of that powder. It's the middle of the day, and my nose is getting shiny. Can't win an award looking shiny!"

After a quick touch-up and the resolution of the shiny situation, the word came from the studio that his coverage would be their top story of the day. The station's news team was instructed to stay on scene until there was a resolution.

Chip was to report back anytime something happened and was told that the station would be cutting into shows at the top of each hour to report on the hostage situation. That in addition to any events that occurred that the camera crew could tape. Then the station would run one of those "We interrupt your regularly scheduled programming to bring you …" and it would be whatever footage Chip got off the scene.

With that, the cameraman began the countdown from three to one, and the cameras began rolling.

Chip Rodgers began, "Chip Rodgers reporting on hour two of the hostage situation at Credit Bank. We have found out that there are several men who have entered the branch of Credit Bank. This is not a small operation; there are apparently over a dozen men in there. Usually, a robbery is an in-and-out job. The fact that we have entered the second hour of a robbery and that the assailants are still in there is a concern for the local police force. They have not issued a comment yet, but I suspect with a robbery of this magnitude there will be a negotiator called in soon. Stay tuned to Channel 5 News for all the coverage."

Daniel Smith was not the typical clean-cut teenager. He had long ago embraced the Goth lifestyle and wore black clothing, white face makeup, and black eyeliner. He had been content to be the alternative kid who not many people spoke to. He had a few good friends and strangely enough a good relationship with his parents. He had counted on being Goth for his whole high school career. What he had not counted on was the raging hormones that consumed him, or the attention of the high school cheerleader Stacey Wilcox. Stacey had been consumed by her love of Edward in a certain four-book saga romance involving vampires and werewolves. So Stacey took to liking the brooding, quiet, pale guy in her science class, linking the experience to the first meeting of the two lovers in the book. Daniel, of course totally unaccustomed to the attention of girls, much less gorgeous cheerleaders, proved to be the "doting, totally in love, can't be apart boyfriend" Stacey dreamed off. So they had started a romance, much to the disbelief of the general student body. He wrote her love letters, drove her home after practices, and even snuck into her room at night so they could sleep together. And true to the story, they only slept platonically, no hanky panky until they got married. Daniel believed they would of course. He was a smart kid, destined to go to big places. He had received early admission to a prestigious university. He planned to make a career in the technology field, maybe as a developer. He figured that he would be making a six-figure salary by the time he was in his late twenties. Stacey would be the perfect wife, and he would continue to dote on her and take care of her. She could do whatever she wanted, philanthropy work, continue as a cheerleader coach, or even become a stay-at-home mom. Daniel beamed at that thought, his Stacey taking care of their little children. He thought how great coming home to her every night would be some not-too-distant day in the future.

In the present, he was concluding his senior year of high school. Daniel usually got to school long before sunrise to work on the school's morning radio show. He would stay after school in the library until it closed, finishing his homework. Even though Daniel was Goth and slightly antisocial, he still dreamed of getting a college education and moving away from the crowds in his high school. He was going to move out east and enjoy his life as a college student and embrace all the diversity that college embodied. He would not be viewed as strange or slightly scary, as he was at school. Prior to vampires becoming cool, he was nicknamed "The Vamp" and was made fun of for it—until he started dating Stacey. Stacey was the be all and end all in popularity, and once she started dating Daniel, all the social taboos around him were erased. The Vamp became a term of endearment, a cool nickname for him. He and Stacey were the "it" couple.

Their romance had lasted since November of last year. It had been a long, rainy winter, and they were happy to spend as much time as possible together. Over the summer, he had gotten a job at a local rock radio station as a production assistant. Stacey spent her days at the beach or scouting schools that she wanted to attend. In the evenings, they would meet up and watch movies, drink, or do whatever else couples in love did when spending their last summer together. With one week left together, Stacey had decided to make it special. Yes, that kind of special. The "going-all-the-way" special. She borrowed her parents' cabin on a secluded island near the city. It was not the type of cabin that comes to mind, one of those small cabins in the middle of the woods with one room and an outhouse in the back. No, this resembled more of a chalet; it was multi-level, covered in glass that overlooked spectacular views of the ocean. It was the perfect setting for "special evenings."

Stacey had planned it out to the last detail. She went to the grocery store and came back with her car's trunk full of delicious food. She put the perishables like the fruits and veggies, red velvet cake, and pre-cooked lobster in the fridge. A bottle of champagne and chocolate-dipped strawberries were placed within easy reach for the big night. She stocked the pantry full of yummy goodies, ensuring they would be content all weekend.

In the guestroom where the magic was going to happen, she ensured the mood was set, arranging candles that she planned to light that night. There was even sheer, white fabric draped over the four-poster bed and luxurious Egyptian sheets for them to crawl into. She did not disturb the master bedroom that belonged to her parents. Luckily they were not joining her and Daniel that weekend. With the kitchen stocked and the bedroom set for romance, she felt content and confident that everything would go perfectly for them that evening.

With a few hours to kill before sunset, Stacey planned on frolicking in the water and maybe encouraging her boyfriend to get a tan. He was just so pale; she thought maybe a little color would look good on him.

That day was extremely sunny and hot. It was a record breaker in terms of temperature, and Stacey had insisted they go out and enjoy it. Daniel was less than keen on going out, as he had avoided the sun for most of his high school career. It had bothered him. He ended up getting heat rashes very quickly for some reason. But out of love for his girlfriend, he put on some SPF 15; it was the highest protection Stacey had at the cabin. Together they walked down to the beach. He put the towel down on the sand and headed out into the water. He and Stacey splashed around and then went out for a swim. When they returned to shore, Muffin, Stacey's Sheltie dog, was waiting for them. She was wagging her tail and giving them a look that was begging for a walk. Stacey mentioned that she was going to take Muffin out for a bit. After the exertion of the long swim, Daniel settled down to take a nap. He settled in the shade of a tree, but as the sun began to move, the shade receded, leaving a sleeping Daniel exposed to the sunlight. Stacey had taken the long route on the island, enjoying the company of her pooch and the warm weather. Her mind was preoccupied with other things, and she forgot she had left her very pale boyfriend on the beach. After a couple of hours, the grumble in her tummy prompted her to go back. She thought about the kitchen where there were all kinds of delicious foods waiting for them. She wondered if Daniel was hungry too. When she arrived at the beach, she saw her boyfriend, extremely red and splotchy. Upon coming closer, she noticed he seemed to be covered in a really bad rash. She thought it best to get him inside, for he looked like he had a bad sunburn. Feeling bad that she had left him alone for so long, she rushed up to him to wake him up.

She began the routine of waking him by kneeling next to him and giving him a kiss. He loved waking up to a kiss by her. This time, nothing. *Strange*, she thought.

"Daniel, honey, time to wake up. Let's go have a late lunch. I am starving!" She looked at him with her beautiful eyes and expected him to wake up to the sound of her voice. He did not stir. She nudged him, but still he did not move. She began to get angry with him. She wondered what kind of game he was playing and just what he expected her to do on the beach in order to wake him up. *Well*, she thought, *he won't be expecting this!* She slapped him with all her might, knowing it would hurt the sunburn! And nothing. He didn't move a muscle.

Sensing the commotion, Muffin came up to Daniel. She sniffed him and started barking up a storm. Stacey grew very concerned; her boyfriend was not moving despite getting his ear barked off and being slapped extremely hard. When she looked at the place where she had hit him, she saw her handprint clearly on his skin; it was not going away. A deep dread filled her stomach. *What if he was dead?* she thought. Stacey tried to wake him again, and it became apparent he was not responding at all. He was either unconscious or, worse yet, dead.

Freaking out, she ran to the dock where her dad kept their speedboat and a phone for emergencies and turned it on. She frantically dialed 911, asking to have an ambulance meet her on the mainland, as there were no doctors, clinics, or hospitals on the secluded island. She dragged her poor boyfriend's body across the deck and shoved him into the boat and then sped the twenty minutes across the stretch of water to the mainland.

On land, the ambulance was waiting for Stacey and Daniel. I was waiting with the paramedics too. It is a lot easier to claim the body on land than make my way to an island and back. The two paramedics got a look at Daniel while he was still in the boat, and one of them whispered to the other so Stacey could not overhear, "That is the most burnt guy I have ever seen. Look how red he is!" To which his partner replied, "That has got to hurt. Better be careful moving him." They climbed into the boat and began administering first aid. They quickly noticed that Daniel was not moving and not responsive to any administered treatment. Originally worried about the pain they would cause him by moving him, they soon realized he would not feel anything even if they threw him overboard. Sadly, this guy was DOA, dead on arrival.

But being professionals and dealing with a teenager, they followed procedure and administered CPR. Then they lifted him off the boat and onto a stretcher and loaded the body into the ambulance. They knew that he was dead, but being paramedics, they needed a doctor to pronounce. That was the only reason they were taking him to the hospital.

Meanwhile, Stacey was frantic. She had loaded her boyfriend onto the boat but did not check on him in the twenty minutes it took to drive the boat to land. Now she demanded to know what was going on with her boyfriend. She was not leaving while he needed her. One of the paramedics gently said that due to his skin burn and rash, it looked like he may have been allergic to the sun. It was also possible he had suffered sunstroke. "Miss, due to his photosensitivity and what may have been sunstroke, he likely died on the island. There was nothing you could do. You rushed him over here, but we cannot save him."

Daniel looked shell-shocked looking down at his lobsterlike self. He was silent, taking the scene in. He stood motionless, his mouth in an O shape, a mixture of shock and disbelief. But the "nothing you could do" comment from one of the paramedics jarred him. In a flash, he snapped out of hic catatonic state and got angry.

Nothing you could do, Stacey? Nothing she could do? She could have woken me up! She could have not dragged me out onto the beach! I was a pale white dude! What did you think would happen, Stacey? I would just get a gorgeous tan? What the hell?

He stopped yelling at her, which of course didn't help anything because she couldn't hear him now that he was dead. Instead he began to pace with a panicked look on his face.

I can't be dead! I am starting school next week. I got into Yale for heaven's sake. I am set for a dorm room and have my classes picked out. I did not just die on a beach on some forsaken island with a blonde cheerleader bimbo!

"Afraid you did," I said.

He turned and looked at me with a stunned expression and asked, "Who are you?"

"Universally, I am acknowledged as the Reaper. I help people who have recently died pass on and go to the afterlife."

"So you are here to help me deal with my grief and find peace in this situation?"

"Not exactly. I am kind of on the lower end of the pay scale and low on the totem pole in terms of organization. I don't have the training to help deal with your theological issues and grief; we have people for that. I am kind of like a deliveryman. I show up, take you to your designated processing center, and they take care of the rest. Don't worry, they will sort it all out."

"What do you mean processing center?" Daniel asked.

Here we go again, the question that I get asked for the umpteenth time. I wish that the guys in marketing would just make a short brochure or something that we could pass out. It could outline the steps from death to processing to the ever after. Alas, management had not approved that in all their years on the job.

I could tell this could stretch out and be a long conversation. I remembered this kid had a 4.0, he was smart, well-read, and was planning on taking philosophy and computer science courses. He was a thinker. He was going to overanalyze everything and question all meaning. I would have to keep it concise; I was on a schedule here. So I gave him the speech. It was perfected after nearly a century on the job.

"The planet has seven billion people on it. You are one of those seven billion. Each person has his or her own beliefs and has lived in his or her own way on the planet. At some point, each person has thought about his or her death, maybe during a funeral or a sad movie or something. At that point, he or she makes a decision about what he or she would like their afterlife to look like. Some want to fade into space, and others want to be reincarnated right away. Some fade into blackness, and others have an idea of heaven full of their loved ones. Our Customer Service Department hears that thought. It is like a call to them; they write it down and file it. When the time comes, they pass it along to our Preparation Department that makes the arrangements. At processing, you are checked in and debriefed on your life. From there, you are escorted to your afterlife, just as you created it when you thought about it."

I took a breath to personalize the speech now. "I see here you are destined for Yale! A respected institution. The one in your afterlife comes complete with a bunch of dead philosophical guys that you can trade ideas with. There is even a founder of computers up there, so you will have your college experience, just not technically among the living. Capish?"

"Oh, so that is how it all works. Interesting. The afterlife is generally subjective."

"Pretty much. Ready for the processing center?"

"Yale, here I come!"

Chapter Three: 3:00 p.m.

B REAK TIME. I LOVE BREAK TIME. I LOVE THE SCONES IN the break room and the fizzy, bubbly sodas in the vending machines. I love being able to kick back and relax for a little bit. I had transitioned Daniel, one nouveaubody (NB). Seeing as I let Kevin have a few extra hours on the planet, I would need to find a time to collect him in the evening.

While sipping my soda and chomping down on my raspberry and white chocolate scone, I reflected on my day. It had started out with the announcement of my retirement. Karl was full of it as always, and Deborah was her friendly, happy self as always. Now that I was retiring, it might be a good day to ask her out. I would no longer be violating the company policy of employees dating. I was retiring, she was working, it would be all-good. I looked around the break room hoping to see her, but no luck. I made a mental note to ask her out at lunch. I crumpled up my soda can and threw it in the recycling. I dusted the crumbs off my clothes and headed out of the break room.

Time to head out and collect my next NB. Looking at the footnote, it seemed like she was going to be difficult and have a very interesting death.

"Chip Rodgers here at the scene at Credit Bank. Those of you who have tuned in since the beginning of this crisis know that the bank was entered by several men at 1:00 p.m. this afternoon. Since then, we have learned that there are at least a dozen men holding up the bank branch here at Credit Bank. These men have apparently dispersed themselves throughout the building and may be holding each floor hostage. There are over a thousand employees within the building behind me." He touched his earpiece. "I am just getting some new information. Apparently there is a police negotiator being brought in to talk to the robbers. Can we get a shot? There he is in the suit ..."

Emmie Guggliatti was planning a party for her two daughters, Rita, six, and Clarissa, four. Being from a well-to-do family, Emmie had spared no expense. She had three cakes, each at $1,000. These were made by one of those shops featured on the Food Network, one that specialized in creating ornate and elaborate cakes. There was a buffet of snacks, including popcorn, artisan chips, and gourmet chocolate. She had pizza, hot dogs, and an entire circus-themed party. That was for the kids. For the adults at the party, she had a smoothie station set up. She served a low-carb lunch and had a seafood station filled with king crab, fresh oysters, and other seafood. She also had a sushi chef making handmade creations.

Her husband's variety of businesses had done very well in the past year, so the budget for the birthday party was one hundred thousand dollars. Some of that went to the couture outfits each member of the family was wearing. There was also staffing for the event. A large part of the budget went to the circus act that she had hired. And finally a part of it went to the goodie bags, which included a miniature gold elephant in commemoration of the party. A Russian circus would come in, complete with elephants, birds, and the highlight of the evening—a tiger! It would be the most talked-about event of the season.

That was very important to Emmie—that everything was lavish, expensive, and would be talked about. She was a housewife. Not the stay-home, 1950s', cleaning-the-house-and-making-her-husband-dinner-as-soon-as-he-came-home type, complete with a glass of brandy and a cigar. Side bar: I wish I was alive for that era. No, she was not that kind of wife. Emmie was the one in charge. She ran a tight ship in her house. She was the housewife who belonged in gated communities, living in lavish mansions, and from what I hear, she would fit perfectly on television reality shows. Her husband, Mike, owned a few gas stations and convenience stores, and a construction business as well. He made a lot of money, and Emmie spent a fair share of it.

Emmie was a hard woman to like. She liked to yell a lot and throw her considerable weight around. Literally! A bottle blonde, she was the example of new money who liked to flaunt it. Her husband's businesses had gotten them a house in the British Properties, the most exclusive neighborhood in the city. Their white-pillared house decorated in marble boasted seven thousand square feet and a $5.6 million price tag. She had a full closet of designer shoes and handbags. Being a size eighteen, she did not have a lot of high-end designer clothing, but still, most of it came from the exclusive shops around the city that did carry above-average sizes with a designer label.

She liked to be in charge and bossed everyone around. She had already fired three party planners for not listening to her demands. Demands that included, "I want to make the popcorn at the party. Maybe I could get a machine." This rather than just serving the popcorn already specially delivered from the gourmet shop.

Her latest demand was that she actually perform with the circus act. At this, her current party planner, who was a strong woman who had survived life behind the Iron Curtain and took no bull from anyone, looked at her and exclaimed, "Good luck with that. These acts are hard, and I do not think you can pull it off." She could not get on the trapeze, for she could not get her legs to hold on to the bar. On the spinning ring, she got dizzy and almost got sick. Finally trying the silk drapes, she just got tangled. She demanded that the performers find her an act that she could do. The Russian circus performers just scratched their heads and wondered about the woman's sanity.

Finally, a couple of days before the party that was scheduled for Friday, she had the idea that since she was throwing the whole party anyways, she may as well entertain everyone as the ringmaster! So she called up the Russian circus and told them that she would be hosting the whole party as the ringmaster and she would be controlling the acts as well. Her performers were dismayed with the idea and saw it ending in disaster. But she insisted! It was her idea to bring in the tiger. She had the idea that an elephant and chimps were not enough for her party; she also wanted a tiger, as she just *loved* cats!

So scouting for a tiger the circus went and agreed to rent an elderly tiger from the zoo. An additional fee was given to the circus in order to train the tiger to do some tricks. Coupled with the rent fee, this set her back another $30,000, but she did not care. She was not content to have the tiger just sitting in a cage; she wanted him to jump through a flaming hoop. The circus trainer tried to explain that the tiger was a captive animal from the zoo; he was not a performer accustomed to doing tricks. Emmie refused to listen and demanded that the trainer teach him to jump through the hoop and whatever else would look good.

On the day of the rehearsal, the performers somehow coaxed him to jump through hoops, but they would not set them on fire. Emmie of course insisted that the hoops be lit and the tiger jump through the damn fire. The circus performers advised Emmie against it. The party planner pleaded with Emmie not to do it. When she refused to give up the notion, the planner made sure that the check for her fee had cleared. It had, so she gave up trying to make Emmie see the absurdity of having a live tiger jump through a flaming hoop at a kids' party.

The stage was set for a beautiful party, all glittery and pink. The decorations were up. The ice sculpture was displayed, still frozen and not showing any signs of melting yet. Moms were driving up the U-shaped driveway in their BMWs and Range Rovers. All of them got out of the cars with their legs tanned, their eyes behind expensive designer sunglasses. They went up to the house, greeted by the spectacle that was Emmie's party. They went through the marbled entrance, through the gourmet kitchen, and into the backyard, which was decorated as a circus. A trapeze was suspended, and performers were flying through the air performing stunts. There was a gentleman lying on a bed of nails. A contortionist was bending every which way. A fire breather was right by the hotdog stand, delighting kids by burning the dogs. A couple of monkeys were serving juice boxes throughout the party, and a snake charmer was weaving through the party with her giant python. It was a spectacle to be seen. In the corner of the yard stood a solitary cage, and pacing in it was the tiger that was to be the main attraction at the party.

After the snacks were served, the food was eaten, the cake was devoured, and the kids were at the perfect pitch of squeals and sugar highs, the main event took place. The drumroll rolled, and out came Emmie, dressed in a glittering red-and-gold sequined outfit. She made a show of walking to the cage and releasing the tiger. The parents quickly went to their kids and scooped them up in case they needed to run in a hurry. The kids were delighted. The tiger was oblivious. He was born and bred at the zoo; he had seen kids all his life and had no interest in them. Emmie made the motion for him to do a loop around her, which he obligingly did with an uninterested yawn. After completing that, she gave him a treat. She beckoned him to speak, and he did so with a loud roar. The kids squealed in delight. She motioned him to the chair, and he jumped up. Then she held out the hoop, and obligingly, he jumped through it. The kids cheered and clapped. Emmie beamed with pride. She was the star attraction at the party. This was a fantastic party, and it would be the talk of the town for years to come, she knew. She triumphantly cried out, "And now for his great trick, Tommy the Tiger will jump through the ring of fire!" The crowd at the party was abuzz with anticipation; their excitement had hit peak level. All little eyes were on the tiger and Emmie as she lit the ring on fire. The parents could not believe this was happening at the party, and they wondered how they would be able to top this spectacle at their kids' parties.

The ring crackled with fire, and Emmie told the tiger to jump! And nothing happened. He cocked his head to the side, looked at her and the flaming ring before him, and looked away. It was like he was saying there was no way that he would be jumping through that. Emmie shouted at him once more, "Jump through the ring!"

The tiger was not interested in following Emmie's instruction and did not make the effort to jump. So Emmie decided to give him a little motivation by smacking him with her whip. The tiger had had enough of her. He pounced off his chair and landed on Emmie. And then he began to maul her. The delighted squeals of the children turned to screams of terror at the first sight of blood. The parents rushed to cover their kids' eyes and ran for the exits. There way chaos as there was a mass exodus of parents running for their lives away from the tiger and his victim.

Of course the reaction of the performers was absolute horror at Tommy the Tiger's mauling a woman. But none of them really made a huge effort to get the tiger off Emmie. Certainly no one wanted to shoot or harm the beautiful animal, figuring if one of them had to be hurt, it may as well be Emmie. It took the tiger thirty seconds to kill Emmie. Once he finished, he sat there contently licking his right paw. He looked peaceful, like it was just another grooming day. Of course the mangled body of the woman next to him stood reminder of what had happened. Emmie's husband was horrified at first but then realized that Emmie had a huge life insurance policy and that this would most certainly qualify as an accidental death. He was sure that he would be an even richer man after this episode. He would find love again, he thought. Yes, it could all work out.

Emmie was less than pleased to have been killed off. She could not believe that her perfect party was ruined by that stupid tiger. She knew that the neighborhood and her friends would be talking about this for years, but not in the way she wanted them to. She wanted them to talk about the spectacle, the lavishness, the unbelievable party. Not the mauling. Unfortunately, that would be a topic that would be discussed for a long time. Those who were there would recount it like a war story, telling exactly what they were doing when it happened. But they would leave out how they did nothing to stop it from happening. Yes, it was a mark of pride to have been there and to be able to tell "The Tiger Story."

As for Emmie, when I informed her that she was dead, her speech consisted of pretty much all expletives, and I do not want to repeat them here. It was the loudest, most cuss-filled hour I ever spent, and I got physically assaulted too. I was glad to turn her over to the processing center and wished them luck on dealing with her. Yeah, processing tells the mauling story too. Heck, it is a good one!

Chapter Four: 4:00 p.m.

LET ME EXPLAIN SOMETHING HERE. FOR US IN THE afterlife, time is infinite and not constrained by the devices of man. So while I do have a twelve-hour day in human time, the time spent up here feels very different. I guess it is akin to when you hate doing something, it seems that time passes at a snail's pace, and when you are having an amazing time, it seems to be over in a flash. That is sort of the concept up here; time is fluid, and you make what you want of it. Therefore, if in the middle of a workday when I am supposed to be collecting NBs, I can pop upstairs, get a round of golf in, careful to be back in the human hour when I am supposed to collect, nobody cares. So after a few NBs were collected this day, I decided to head back to corporate and have a nice lunch. It was a pretty good gig with catered lunches served buffet style. I helped myself to some chicken, some salad, and some prime rib. The desserts I plated on another tray, which included crème brule, cheesecake, pecan tart, strawberry shortcake, and vanilla ice cream. I did not want to eat too much. I still had a busy day ahead, including getting the guts to ask out Debbie.

Okay, I will admit it. I don't have game! I learned that phrase from hundreds of people I collected. You have game if you can successfully flirt and end up with someone you like. I do not have that. In life, I only had one relationship. It was with my wife.

When I passed, she and my child were all I thought about, but I was told by my reaper that they would not come for at least fifty years. I was happy that they would live good, long lives, but I was looking forward to seeing them again.

The hardest thing I ever had to do was make the transition for my wife. We had gotten married when I was nineteen and she was seventeen. We had been dating for a year, and in the course of it, she got pregnant. It was a different time, and we got married. I was twenty-one with a two-year-old son when I got drafted for the war. Twenty-three when I passed away. My kid had not seen me while I was on the front. The two years apart made an impact, and I don't think he remembered me. That was hard. I loved my wife, and she stayed faithful while I was alive, but she moved on after I died. A soldier had come back from the front wounded. He lived in our neighborhood, and they took comfort in each other. At first they got to just talking, then going for walks, and eventually dinners at each other's homes. In less than a year, they got married. They were in love for fifty-one years when she passed away. Seeing her aged after so many years was a shock for me. For her, I was a difficult memory, one she did not want to face. She said that she had loved me years ago, but it was not true love, not anything like the love she shared with her husband, Ken. They had gone on to have three more children, and he adopted my son. At that moment, I realized that while she may have been my true love, I was not hers. She told me that she hoped to continue her life with Ken when he passed, and she apologized for not wanting to be with me. It was like losing her all over again.

A few years later, my son passed away, and he did not recognize me at all. Nor did he acknowledge me when I told him I was his father. He knew Ken as his dad. I had hoped that I would get a good reaction from my family when we were finally reunited. I thought they would want to have something to do with me in the afterlife. In reality, they did not. They had moved on. They had moved on without me. So though my initial service of fifty human years was up, I reenlisted for another fifty, which was coming to a close today. Time flies in a very different way up here, and the second fifty years were good ones.

I fared better with my parents than with my wife and son. Years earlier, my parents were happy to see me. My mom cried, and my dad gave me a hug. They even asked me to come live with them. That was not in the cards, so instead I make a point of visiting them often. They live in a part akin to Boca Raton in Florida, and they wear a lot of white and play canasta and shuffleboard.

However, my own family disappointed me and made me want to focus only on work. Solitude became my friend. I requested to not transition anyone I had known or was related to. I lived with that disappointment for a long time. I did not date in the afterlife. Dating is hard, even in the afterlife. I had only recently developed a crush on Debbie. I had no idea how to act on it!

Now was as good a time as any. Lunchtime, I timed it so I could take my break around the same time that Debbie does. I had to know one way or another if she would go out with me, and if I saw her, I vowed to ask her out.

Making my way through the seating area, I saw a variety of groups sitting together. In one group, I spotted Deborah, or "Little Debbie" as I secretly nicknamed her because she is so sweet like the treat! I passed by and gave her a polite smile, thinking, *Don't look creepy, don't look geeky, don't look too much! Damn it, looked too much! Move, move, move, head to the back—there is an empty table!*

Once seated at the table, I started in on my lunch and felt the presence of someone. To my surprise, Debbie was standing over my table, and she demurely looked down on me and asked, "May I sit down and share a treat?" She looked over at my dessert tray. To be frank, I had only really grabbed enough dessert for one person, but this was my golden opportunity to get to know her a little better, so I was not passing this up. She sat down and helped herself to my crème brule. *Darn it. I really wanted that one.* Then I remembered I could just get one later. Now was the time to focus on Debbie, not dessert. *By the end of the conversation, I might even get the courage to ask her out.*

She looked thoughtful, as if wondering what to say. "So what's your favorite movie?" she asked me awkwardly.

"*City of Angels!*" I quickly replied. "I love Nicolas Cage. Man, that guy just defines acting."

She looked relieved to have found a topic and said, "*City of Angels* is actually based on a true story. It happened to Larry from Terminal Diseases."

"No way! Are you kidding me? It is based on one of our guys? That is wild! How did the humans even hear about it?"

"When he became human again, he realized he was on the planet with no skills and no education, so he figured why not write his love story in a screenplay and get some money doing that. I mean, he didn't really want to be a kept husband by the doctor forever."

"Makes sense," I responded.

"You know, you are very different than I expected. I thought you would be this super macho guy who is into violence and action movies. When I asked you about your favorite movie, I thought you would respond with *Jarhead* or *Black Hawk Down*."

I wondered what she meant by that. Did she think I was a tough guy before and liked me because of it? Or did she have a thing for guys who died in combat? Did she want an alpha male type or was she in fact just giving me a backhanded compliment?

Either way, I did not have another day on the job to find out the answer to that. Today I was scheduled to retire, and I would not have time to flirt and then hope that down the road she liked me. I had to find out if there was any romantic possibility for us. I needed to lay my cards on the table.

"Debbie, I call you Debbie, not Deborah, because you are sweet like snack cakes. And I have a sweet tooth."

Oh man, that sounded incredibly lame and corny out loud! Okay, power through it. Get your feelings out there, I thought.

"There is a time for bravery. I jumped on the grenade that killed me to save my troops. That can be seen as brave, but it can also be seen as stupid. I never met my son because of it. But fighting in a bloody war and doing this job, seeing the things we reapers see, it becomes too much. When my job is over, I want to relax. I want to watch sappy romance movies and laugh at comedies. My piece of paradise is on a lake where the fish are always biting and where I can relax by the fire with a good book. That is the kind of guy I am. If you think you could like that guy, then I would love to take you out on a date. If I am not your type, then starting tomorrow you never have to see me again."

"Pick me up tomorrow at seven for a movie?" she replied. I smiled and nodded. With that, I got up and headed out the cafeteria. I tried to look cool and collected, but as soon as I was out of the line of sight, I did a little happy dance.

On my way out of the cafeteria I passed a television set with Chip Rodgers saying, "Get a shot of that! Get a shot! Get that shot!" People on camera were coming out of the building. Chip angled himself to be in the shot, with his back to the hostages coming out of the building. "Chip Rodgers at the scene. What we are seeing here are some of the hostages who have been through this horrifying ordeal being released outside. Their families must be so relieved to see them out those doors and coming home to them this weekend. You are seeing the first footage of the released hostages right here, ladies and gentlemen. We at Channel 5 are exhaling a collective sigh of relief. Stay tuned. We are going to cover every minute of this ongoing crisis."

James Stamford was a stockbroker for twenty years before the crash. He had accumulated a lot of wealth during that time and had enough to live a life of leisure for a little bit. He had amassed considerable wealth in his years in the corporate rat race and did not feel the need to stick around after the global crisis that occurred in the summer of 2008. He thought he would go back once the market recovered, but after a few years of a bad economy and him losing interest, he decided to start a new career as an account executive for the local news station. He enjoyed selling commercial airtime and had a lot of fun at his job.

That was most of the time. Today was a bit of an exception.

Where are the commercials? he wondered.

Ever notice that during a special report there are no commercials? It is uninterrupted coverage. It happens during a special address by the president. It happens when there is coverage of some disaster in the Midwest. All eyes are glued on the reporter or speaker, and there are no interruptions of any kind. Especially not of jingles and ads asking you to buy something. Most people do not notice that. Unless that person makes their living off selling commercials. That was the case with James. He worked for Channel 5. He was their account executive, which is the title for the person convincing businesses to buy airtime to air their commercials. Today Channel 5 was busy airing the biggest story they ever had. With every commercial that was not airing during the special report, James cringed.

He would have to place those commercials that did not air during a later time, which was going to be a lot of work. That or lose money if he did not place the commercials. Which meant a reduced commission check. As the hours ticked by, he began to get angrier and angrier with the situation. He was losing money. When the first hour went by with the special report and no commercials, he thought that it was good for business to be the only station breaking the news. He could use that as a selling point for a few months to come. But when it went into the second hour, he began to worry. He called his general manager, stating that they could still air commercials when nothing was happening.

The station manager laughed at him, saying, "Nothing is happening? We have a situation downtown! A hostage situation! That stuff never happens, and we were the first to cover it! Do you know the amount of eyeballs we have on our station? The ratings boosts we are getting? There is no way I am compromising that in order to air a cat food commercial and miss the building blowing up in those thirty seconds!" With that, she hung up on James.

So despite his best efforts, there was nothing else he could do.

The only thing that calmed him down during stressful situations was diving. Out there in the ocean, it was peaceful. There were no distractions.

James shared his beachside house with his son, Jake, an eighteen-year-old privileged kid who had not yet decided whether to go to college (his dad's ambition) or go backpacking through Southeast Asia with his girlfriend. The choice was clear for Jake. He wanted to go to travel, but James was threatening him with disinheritance if he chose that option. James wanted Jake to go to his university and join his fraternity. Jake would be a shoo-in as a legacy for the fraternity. James gave a generous donation to the university to make sure his son would get in. He thought that Jake would have a blast partying and drinking at school. He just wanted Jake to get a degree. It did not matter what kind; Jake just needed that piece of paper. James would ensure that Jake would have no problem finding a job with one of his friends' firms. Also, James hoped Jake would find other girls and forget about the girlfriend he was currently dating.

She was definitely from the wrong side of the tracks. James had heard that her dad was in prison for homicide. He had hoped that last part was a rumor. It wasn't! Unluckily for James, his son's girlfriend was very close with her father, and they often shared ideas. One of these ideas she had decided to share with Jake.

Jake and James had gone on vacation to the Caribbean the year before and had gone snorkeling. Both enjoyed themselves. When Jake came back home, he enrolled in some diving classes and found it really enjoyable to be underwater in the ocean. There was a lot of marine life under there, and his favorite experience was encountering the occasional octopus. When his dad noticed that Jake was spending a lot of time in the water, he bought an old boat that was no longer fit to sail and decided to sink it in the cove near their house. This provided a habitat for some of the creatures underwater. Often there would be fish swimming through the boat, and there were plenty of shellfish that made the wreckage their permanent home. This summer, Jake had finally convinced his dad to try diving. To his surprise, James actually enjoyed it. Going out with his son and seeing the underwater world was a bonding experience. James decided to ask Jake if he wanted to join him for an afternoon dive. Jake declined, saying he had to finish packing before the barbeque and getting some last-minute supplies. Pushing his luck, James asked him what he was packing for and got the very pleasant answer, "college."

He knew better than to be overly excited in front of this particular teenager, so he shook his hand and congratulated him on the decision.

He also left him a hundred dollars to get some extra things for the barbeque.

The past week, Jake was pretty busy spending his time with his girlfriend. Tomorrow he was hosting a going-away barbeque. James made a mental note to try to get in some time with his son before he left the nest.

James got ready for his solo dive. He checked his oxygen tank. It read full, and he shimmied into his wetsuit. He placed the goggles over his eyes, the flippers over his toes, and got the breathing apparatus ready. He waddled over to the water in his wetsuit and flippers. When he was a bit further in, James began to submerge. He was glad to be in the water on this record-breaking scorching day. He had decided to dive over to the boat to see what kind of life was there today. James had really begun to enjoy himself by the time he neared the boat. He decided to go in and explore it today. The inside of the submerged boat was full of a school of fish that looked like sardines. He was marveling them when he began to feel a little lightheaded. He thought that was odd. He checked his tank meter and saw that it was more than halfway full. He figured maybe it was the depth, or maybe he was claustrophobic being in the boat. He decided that maybe it was time to head back.

Unfortunately, that was not the plan Jake and Elisa had for him. They had hatched it out together and waited on shore until they saw James dive over to the submerged boat. They could see the trail of bubbles on the surface of the water that led in that direction. Once they knew he was headed that way, they suited up and followed him in. The two divers came up behind James, and one pulled on the hose that connected the oxygen tank to his mouthpiece and yanked the mouthpiece out. This released the precious oxygen into the water. James began to panic and thrash around, trying to get the mouthpiece back in. Unfortunately, with the depth that he was in, the pressure in his ears was too much, and that only added to his panic. His lungs were burning, his ears were feeling like they would explode, and he could not reach the mouthpiece to put it back in. He thrashed for thirty more seconds before he let the water into his mouth and stopped thrashing. Elisa swam up to him when he had been still for a minute. She calmly put the mouthpiece back into his mouth. She and Jake knew the tank was almost empty. They had tampered with the meter. James was going in with a quarter tank of oxygen prior to his dive even though it read full. He was not going to be able to make it back even if Jake and Elisa had not intervened. But Elisa insisted they make sure everything went according to plan.

Once they were sure that James was dead, they decided to cut one of the weights on him so that he would surface eventually when sufficiently bloated. The couple then calmly swam back to the shore. They put away their suits and tanks and went into the house. Once there, Jake got onto his Facebook and went to the event page, announcing his going-away barbeque. Here he saw that thirty-four of his friends would be attending, and he wrote: *Can't wait to see you all before I head off to college! Bring booze and babes.* The plan was to host the barbeque as planned and then, during the party, act worried that he had not seen his dad in a couple of days. Elisa would suggest calling the authorities, stating that she knew his dad would want to be at home to make sure the party did not get out of control. Also, he would want to say good-bye to his son prior to going to college. The authorities would be called, with plenty of witnesses to see Jake worried about his dad. Once James was found, Jake would act devastated and decide he could not go to college after his dad's death. He would announce that he needed time to get himself together. Maybe go to Southeast Asia and travel for a bit.

He knew he was entitled to his inheritance of two-plus million. He also figured he would get half the profits from the house sale. The other would go to his mother who was currently living in Las Vegas. So he guessed as an eighteen-year-old kid, he would soon be getting five million. Not a bad way to start off his life.

James was pretty dismayed when I picked him up. "My own son killed me. For money and his girlfriend."

I sighed and said, "Trust me, it is not the first time I have seen someone kill for money or love. In this case, it is both. You were right to be concerned; it was her idea, and she planned most of it. They are going to go on a nice trip thanks to the money they will get from your 'accidental death.' You made him the only beneficiary there, right?"

"Right! Who dangles that much money in front of an eighteen-year-old kid? I am an idiot!"

"Not as big of one as your son. Elisa only plans on being with him a little bit longer. Then she plans on getting half the money by getting pregnant and forcing him to marry her and then divorcing him. Or she might want it all and try to off him too. She hasn't decided yet; she is tossing both ideas in her head. So I can't tell you what will happen."

"Oh my God, I have to warn him! I have to stop him from being with that gold digger!"

"Take it up with our Worldly Communications Department. They will be able to arrange for you to visit your son in a dream. Maybe even for some signs to be sent. You may want to petition them for recurring nightmares for her as well so that she maybe has a change of heart about using your son. Come. I will put you in touch with them."

Chapter Five: 5:00 p.m.

DUNCAN CRABAPPLE, A PARTNER AT THE MOST PRESTIGIOUS law firm in town, was heading out of work early. Accustomed to seventy-hour workweeks, the man had a tumultuous marriage and a hag of a wife who he did not like coming home to. However, being as she had put him through law school and kept good records of their income, he knew that divorcing her would cost him a small fortune. So he worked more, saved up money, and then made up excuses to go to conferences at exotic destinations. He would check the Internet to see if there was some sort of conference or lecture that he could claim to be attending while he was really enjoying the company of his longtime girlfriend—a bartender he had met after going for drinks with some of his colleagues after work. She had a big rack, blonde hair, and looked like a former supermodel. She had an eight-year-old son who he bribed with lots of toys, candy, and occasionally cash. It was a good arrangement. He owned a condominium downtown that he claimed to be renting out. In reality, his girlfriend lived there free of charge. He would see her after work before her shift started, spend some time with her, and then head to the wife. Just now, he was sneaking out of work early for a quickie prior to heading up to the cottage with the wife and his two daughters, Anastasia and Tiffany. It had become a bit of a tradition to do a weekend at the cabin before the girls headed up to school, and he usually put on a smile and a happy air while he counted down the hours until the week was over and he could go back to his posh condo in the city.

He was able to get away early today because of the holdup in the bank. Credit Bank was a lucrative client, and the law firm was consumed by the story of their being held hostage. HR had sent out e-mails and memos asking the lawyers to hope for the safe resolution to the crisis and to prepare for contingencies. By the middle of the afternoon, it had become obvious that the productivity level of the firm had decreased. Some of the lawyers were consumed by worry about the people on the news and tuned in to every report by Chip Rodgers. Others were just anxious to get started on the weekend and used the crisis as an excuse to leave early. Apparently everyone could come up with a neighbor or a teller or someone they knew who was affected by the crisis, so they just had to leave work. It was a crock, for most did not know people there, but it was a great way for them to leave and get the weekend started early. Even the lawyers who worked with the bank knew only the litigants and those they sent the invoices to. Most of the concern was about making sure the checks would keep coming.

Duncan had acted appropriately all day and kept the staff morale up, but toward the end of that particular Friday, he dismissed the staff for the day and asked them to be back early on Monday. He then arranged a meeting with his girlfriend. As he was leaving, the offices on his floor stood abandoned. He did not really pay attention to the newscast when it warned about the power outage that was going to occur on the grid that his building was part of. He most certainly did not pay attention when the warning was being broadcast again when he paged the elevator. Instead, he was busy popping a blue pill and fantasizing about his afternoon delight.

Now, had Duncan listened to the newscast by Chip Rodgers, he would have heard the news: "Chip Rodgers here. There has been progress in the Credit Bank hostage crisis. The SWAT team has decided to try to infiltrate the building. The buildings within the two-block radius of Credit Bank have been evacuated. Also, since it is a Friday and it is late in the afternoon, most workers will have gone home for the day from the business district. The city will be cutting the power to the grid in order to allow the SWAT members to enter the building in the cover of darkness. All persons in the power grid from Main Street to Central Street and from First to Seventh Avenues are encouraged to either leave the area or be prepared to hunker down with no power.

Duncan got on that elevator and pressed the lobby button. The elevator doors closed, and he went down one floor before the power shut down. The elevator stopped with a screeching halt, and Duncan was thrown off balance. "What the hell?" He looked at the elevator buttons. None were lit up, and the elevator's brightness was reduced to the red glow of the emergency light. He got a little worried at this point. Duncan was terrified of small, confined spaces, and with the elevator going dark, he suddenly realized he was sitting in a death trap. He envisioned the brakes failing and the elevator plunging to the ground where the impact would reduce him to a crushed man barely identifiable by modern forensic measures. He wondered how much air was available in the elevator, and would he suffocate? Then he remembered that he could be rescued. All he had to do was pick up the emergency phone and call. When he got an answer, he said, "I am trapped in an elevator and need someone to come get me out."

In response, he was told, "Sir, I am sorry, but you need to calm down. We have most of the police and fire personnel dealing with the hostage crisis. We have cut power to the area as a result of that crisis. Once it is resolved, we will power the grid back up, and the elevator will continue to function normally. We are not able to send anyone to get you. There is simply not enough manpower available." This response incited a lot of cursing from Duncan and the threat to sue everyone and their dogs for this inconvenience! That he would bankrupt their company! And didn't they know who he was? The operator did not. Nor did she seem to care. Her shift was over five minutes ago, and it was time for the weekend. She apologized once more and said there was nothing she could do, and then she hung up the phone. This left Duncan alone in the dark. After half an hour in the small space, Duncan was sweating profusely, panicking, and erect. The pill had apparently kicked in.

I will spare you the thoughts that were running through his head, everything from being with his girlfriend, to what would happen to his family, and a few more morbid thoughts. But overall, the theme was panic; he ended up getting himself completely worked up. After years of long, stressful hours, lack of physical activity, extreme duress, and some "medication," he had a heart attack. It was anguish for five minutes, and then the elevator suddenly became eerily still. No life was aboard it.

The irony of it was that the elevator resumed power ten minutes later. It went down to the lobby as Duncan had instructed it to. The doors opened, and there was Duncan prostrate on the floor. The maintenance guy who was waxing the lobby was the one to see Duncan. He thanked his lucky stars upon finding him before the end of his shift, because had Duncan remained in the elevator over the weekend, he would be dealing with a really stinky mess come Monday. And it is pretty hard to get the smell of three-day-old dead guy out of a small, confined space, even for a professional maintenance man.

Duncan was not happy to see me, as one can imagine. He threatened to sue me too. I told him to do it. I gave him my full name and the location of my gravesite. I wished him luck on suing a guy who had been dead ninety-nine years and was buried in France. He then threatened to sue the corporation I worked for. Again I wished him luck. I stated that they were in charge of his arrangements now that he had passed, and if he thought there was litigation hell on earth with cases being stalled for years, he had not seen anything like it yet. He would be stuck in limbo for decades if he tried to sue them. And ultimately, he would lose.

Duncan for the first time in his life looked confused. Accustomed to having everything his way, being able to talk himself out of anything, and having life work out for him, he was very surprised that here there was absolutely nothing he could do. He resigned himself, and with his head bowed, he asked what was next. I told him that he could argue the case for decades in the Upper Supreme Court and still never come back to life, or that he could go to processing and get the afterlife he always imagined. Unfortunately, I cannot say what that life was. As a lawyer, he had built in so many contingencies and clauses, I had no idea what to read into it. I knew this was going to be a difficult case to decipher, but hey, we had a legal department too. I would just have to let them deal with it.

Chapter Six: 6:00 p.m.

"CHIP RODGERS REPORTING FROM THE BUSINESS DISTRICT where the power has been cut to the Credit Bank corporate offices here on Main Street. SWAT members are preparing to enter the building. There have been about a hundred hostages released already. Negotiators see this as a sign of good faith, but due to the sheer number of people inside the building, SWAT is planning on entering and neutralizing the threat. We hope to see some more hostages heading out of that building. Stay tuned for the progress on this situation."

Chang Wong was a very nice lady. She was the one lady in the cul-de-sac that had candy and treats that kids actually ate. The parents trusted her, and the kids liked her. She was known for giving all the little kids on the street red envelopes for Chinese New Year. Each envelope contained five dollars, and for the kids on the street, that meant a lot since no one else gave them money or treats. In fact, most of the adults just told the kids to stay off their lawns or not to skateboard in their driveway.

Mrs. Wong was enjoying gardening in the early-evening hour. She was on her knees planting when she heard a voice right above her.

"There's only one Love River in the world, right, Mrs. Wong?" At the sound of this, Mrs. Wong looked up from her little garden. Standing there looking at her were two little faces. Both were blonde and green-eyed. One belonged to the little boy Mikey, about three years old. He was eating a Popsicle with bluish water already running down his chubby little fingers. The voice that had spoken was his sister, Maya, five years old and probably the most curious child Mrs. Wong had ever met. They lived next door to the Wongs with their parents and a giant mastiff dog.

Mrs. Wong smiled at the pair and said, "Yes, there is only one Love River. It is located in Taiwan close to the country where I grew up. It was named after a big factory that used to be there called Love Enterprises." She decided to not explain about the folklore of two lovers forbidden by their parents to be together throwing themselves into the river to drown. Legend had it that the locals named the river after them.

"How do you know about the Love River?" Mrs. Wong asked Maya.

"My mommy looked it up on Expedia! I mean ..."

"Encyclopedia?" Mrs. Wong gently inquired.

"Yeah, that's it!" Maya nodded her head. It was then that she pointed to the object in her hand, a postcard. "This postcard says Love River on it! The postman brought it to our house by mistake. Daddy asked me to bring it over to you."

Maya stretched out her hand toward Mrs. Wong and asked, "What are all these funny scribbles on the back? Aren't you supposed to write on a postcard, not draw scribbles?"

Mrs. Wong laughed. "These are letters in my native language. Would you like to know what they say?" Maya nodded her head enthusiastically and handed the postcard over to the elderly lady. She began to read.

> *Dear sister, I am in Kaohsiung Taiwan watching the Dragon Boat Festival on the Love River. It has been a few years since I saw you, and I wish that you were here with me. You remember how as little girls we used to watch the dragon boats go by? Some years later, you remember that time we tried to paddle on one of the boats and nearly fell over into the water? The memories are returning as I am*

watching the races. My son, your nephew, is competing this year, and I wish you were here to see it. I hope to see you soon. Love, your younger sister.

"Wow, dragons live there?" Mikey asked, eyes gleaming.

"Not real live ones, I'm afraid, but there are boats that race on the river. Long boats that have wooden carved dragon heads and tails. That's what the festival is about, racing those dragon boats."

"Boat! Cool! Let's go see Mummy and Daddy and see if we can go see boats." With that, he ran off, and Maya chased after him.

"Wait for me!" she called.

Mrs. Wong still held the postcard in her hand and slowly raised herself into a standing position. She brushed the dirt off her knees with her free hand and decided to head back into the house. The postcard had brought about a rush of memories. She recalled growing up in China as a little girl.

Her father had worked on building the railways that connected big cities throughout North America. He then went back to China and married her mom. As she was growing up, Chang heard stories of skyscrapers and adventures that her dad had. She promised herself that she would one day go visit the cities her dad told her about. In one, she met her husband, Huang Wong, at a dance given by the Chinese Cultural Association. She remembered seeing him in a suit talking to another girl and being just so jealous of her. That girl was talking to the most handsome guy in the room. It turned out that girl was his sister, and she was the one who introduced Chang and Huang. It was after Chang saw her in the bathroom and remarked on how she was talking to the most handsome guy she had ever seen that the girl replied that he was her brother and too shy to talk to anyone else. But if Chang really liked him, she would be happy to introduce them. So it went. They were introduced and spent the whole evening talking. At the end of the evening, he got the courage to ask her for a date. Over the next few months, the shy, handsome man courted her in a dignified and respectful way. By the end of three months, he asked her to marry him. They were married for forty very happy years. During those years, they started a family, bought a home, and traveled the world. He passed away in his sleep one night about ten years ago, and not a night went by when she didn't miss him. The sadness consumed her. In that first year after her beloved Huang passed away, the family worried about her health. Her eldest son worried so much about his mom that he asked her to move in with him and his family.

She was now living with her son and daughter-in-law. She had an upstairs bedroom and tried to stay out of their way, so as to not be a burden. She had a lot of pictures in that room. It was a time capsule of her life, and she loved looking over each of the photos and reminiscing about when they were taken.

There were the ones of her as an attractive, young woman, standing on the Great Wall of China. Then there were the pictures of her and her husband on their wedding day. Also pictures of her kids and grandsons. There was even one of her standing in a pool holding a stingray, taken on her last family vacation to the Dominican Republic.

When she finished looking at her pictures, she took one out of a frame. It was of her and her sister sitting by the water with a dragon boat in the background. She placed the photo in an envelope and wrote her sister a letter to accompany it.

> *Dearest sister, I have received your postcard and the happy news within. I too wish I could be there to celebrate the Dragon Boat Festival. Perhaps we shall see each other soon. Know I keep you in my thoughts and in my heart.*

She placed the letter in the envelope along with the photo. She sealed the envelope shut and placed a stamp on the front. Then she sat down and looked out her window.

She was a woman who had lived a good life and loved her past. But in the present, she was worried about becoming a burden to her family, and her health was not treating her all that well. It was not a big surprise to her then when she was sitting in her favorite rocking chair facing the window where she could see the garden that she had tingles in her left arm, followed by a severe pain in her chest. She sat there and clutched her chest. Her younger grandson came into her room when he heard moans. Randy noticed she was not looking good and ran through the house calling for his dad and mom. They both came to Mrs. Wong and saw that she was struggling to breathe. Randy dialed 911, and the family gathered around the grandmother as she breathed out her last few words. "Children, I have had a good life; do not grieve for my death. Remember, live your life to the fullest, and regret not the things you do but the things you did not do. I will be all right. I am going to go be with Grandpa now." With that, she closed her eyes and passed away.

I get a lot of stories like these, quiet deaths. Some are lucky enough to be surrounded by family in their last moments. Some pass away in their sleep. Others are alone when their last moments come. But many go quietly; in fact, most people simply pass away. T. S. Eliot was right when he said, "This is the way the world ends. Not with a bang but a whimper."

Chapter Seven: 7:00 p.m.

CHIP RODGERS SAID, "OH MY GOODNESS, THERE HAS BEEN a blast from the building. Behind me, you can see the smoke and blown-out windows from the northeast corner of the building. It is believed the emergency escape door was armed with some sort of explosive device, and it has blown out the windows on the floor, and it may have caused some casualties. This is awful. I hope no one was hurt. I will bring you more reports from this building where the hostage negotiation has just taken a horrible turn."

An hour before the explosion, Nancy Grace was asked by her fire chief if she wanted to go to the scene of the hostage situation. It was her day off, and she had just completed her four days on-shift the day before. He stated that he understood if she was not up for it. But she told him she wanted to do it. She was having the kind of day where she needed to get out of her head. It started with a bad dream that she awoke from, and she just could not shake it.

It's funny what one thinks about right after waking from a dream. Some just wake up knowing they dreamed but cannot recall what or who about. Others dream magical things and wake up with a smile after being transported to another world. Still some dream about people that they wish to be with but can't in their waking life, but in dreams they have a magical romance.

When Nancy awoke from her nap that afternoon, she knew exactly what she had dreamt about: her ex-boyfriend Ryan. She vividly saw through his eyes his final battle. He had enlisted in the army right after high school and served two tours. He did not return from the last one. He had been killed by an improvised explosive device detonated while he was doing a sweep of houses.

Nancy remembered vividly the day that the two army soldiers came to her door, dressed in their Class-A uniforms to deliver the news. They visited her and Ryan's parents that day. It was the worst day of her life, seeing them on that doorstep. She had the sinking feeling that they were there to deliver the news that Ryan had been killed in action. But she didn't want to accept it. So she hid. As soon as she saw them through her kitchen window, she crossed the floor and opened the door to the pantry and stepped in. She stayed there in the dark trying to catch her breath. She listened as the two men knocked on her door, first politely and then with urgency. Pound, pound, pound went their fists against her oak door. Then the knocking stopped, and for a moment there was silence. Then one of them spoke. "Guess she's not home. Better let the parents know. We can come back later." As soon as they left, she bolted out of the pantry, knowing her worst fears had been confirmed.

She grabbed the car keys and raced to Ryan's parents' house. She knew his mom would be in distress and inconsolable. She knew she needed to be there for her. She ignored her own feelings of despair, of inconsolable hurt and anger. And she managed to get there before the two soldiers. She managed to grab the inconsolable mother when her knees gave way and she almost collapsed to the floor. She managed to help the family in the worst moment of their lives. That day changed her life forever. She had found her calling, helping people in distress. And so she enrolled at the fire academy and completed her EMT (Emergency Medical Technician) training. She was hired onto the city's fire department within a year of that horrible day. She had been doing that job for five years.

It was her day off, but the nightmare of seeing the images through Ryan's eyes and the memory of him sent shivers down her whole body. It was a distressing dream, and she felt it to be a bad omen. So she went to the only place that made her feel better, to her fire station. There the chief was walking around in circles in his office, talking on the phone. Nancy nodded to Greg in the chief's direction and mouthed, "What's going on?" He got up from the table where he was sitting and motioned her to the other room.

"You haven't heard?" he asked as he closed the door behind them.

"Heard what? I've been asleep all day after getting off-shift."

Greg walked over to the television and turned it on. There on the screen was Chip Rodgers standing downtown. There it was captioned on the screen: a hostage situation. At the bottom of the screen, the ticker was reporting the events in real time. Greg interrupted her reverie. "This has been on TV all day! The chief is talking to the police commissioner about the situation at the bank. He was wondering if this department would be needed." As if on cue, there was an announcement over the PA that all of the staff was to gear up. They would be leaving in ten minutes to head to the situation downtown. At hearing those words, a dread came over Nancy, but she shook it off and went downstairs to put on her gear.

Meanwhile at the scene, Luke Kozlowski and Steve Brown were friends who grew up together. Both their dads were cops, and both of them knew they wanted to grow up just like their fathers. They attended police academy together, and they were assigned to the same precinct. Luke wanted more danger and tougher assignments in his job, so he convinced Steve to join him and apply to SWAT. Luke was the one who loved danger and thrived in these situations. Steve was the calm and rational type who always thought about the consequences of his actions and rarely made split-second decisions. The two men completed their training and were assigned to the same unit again, this time in SWAT. Today they were called to the bank situation. Luke panicked when he heard where he was going, for his wife, Laura, worked there. He and Laura were just married last year. She was the only woman who had managed to tame Luke's philandering heart. Now he loved her with all he had and wanted to start a family. If it had not been for Steve, Luke would have rushed into the bank by himself and tried to rescue her. Steve managed to calm him for a few minutes and ask him to stick to the plan.

SWAT members had been granted access by using a viaduct that they were supposed to climb down through to access the second floor of the corporation. The second floor was vacated earlier, and all the hostages had been released. They were the ones seen on camera as Chip was reporting on their release. The second floor was supposed to be empty, and that was where the SWAT members were to congregate. From there they were to fan out to respective floors. Once on their assigned floors, they were to shoot the robbers and then evacuate the hostages.

All members had been issued night-vision goggles and were hoping to be operating under the cover of darkness. Unfortunately, they were ordered to enter the building early. This was due to the large amount of people still inside the building and the real threat that one of those people would be killed every fifteen minutes until the crisis was resolved.

The bottom line was that the robbers were demanding about $300 million from the bank. Some money had already been paid out, but then the insurance company that covered the bank from damages stated they did not wish to negotiate with terrorists and that they would not be repaying the bank for any monies paid out. That was when the one vacationing senior executive (the CFO) who was not in the building made the executive decision to use force. The bank could not afford to pay the robbers, and therefore they needed SWAT to exterminate them before there were more civilian casualties. So, using some of the darkness that the power company had provided for SWAT, they went in. But it was not completely dark inside, for the windows still let in quite a bit of light.

Luke was worried that the mission would not be a success and that they would not be able to neutralize the threat. He was not assigned to Laura's floor, but he did not trust anyone but himself to get her out safely. So he broke ranks and decided to head down to the main floor where the bank branch was located in order to free his wife. Steve watched him sneak off and followed. When they were clear of other

SWAT members and saw that there was not anyone else around, Steve confronted him and asked what Luke was thinking of doing.

"I am saving my wife's life. No one is going in to get the tellers. They told us to evacuate the other floors first and leave the branch employees for last. If the robbers on that floor get wind of what is happening upstairs, they will shoot up the whole branch, and Laura is in there! I will not let my wife get killed by these guys. Now if you want to help me, come on; otherwise get out of my way because you will not talk me out of this."

Knowing he would not be able to win the argument, Steve conceded and backed his friend up. They had made their way down a floor, and Luke went to open the emergency exit door (sure that the alarm would not sound, as the power was cut off). Unfortunately for him, the door was armed with an Improvised Explosive Device (IED) that detonated as soon as the door was opened. Luke was killed on impact, and Steve was blown back from the blast. He had very severe injuries. He used his radio to call in with, "Ten-thirteen, officer down. I am injured, and my partner has been killed. I need assistance!"

Nancy Grace, the firefighter with five years on the job, heard the distress call. Her instinct to assist a person in need kicked in. She jumped out of the truck and quickly assessed the best way to get in the building. She decided to use the ladder on the truck to access the second floor. She assumed that the windows would be safe to access. She grabbed her EMT bag and climbed up the ladder. Once on top, she broke the window and got inside. She ran in to assist Steve. She made it down to him and performed first aid. He had nasty wounds. There were building fragments in his chest and abdomen, and there were burn patterns on his skin from the explosion. She knew that she would not be able to get him down the ladder by herself and made the decision to drag him out the door. Unfortunately, a second device had been installed that would be detonated with a trip wire should anyone try to exit after the initial explosion. Unfortunately, dragging Steve tripped off that wire. Both Nancy and Steve were killed when that second IED went off.

There are some things even a grim reaper cannot stand to see. In this instance, two police officers who always rushed into danger and made the solemn promise to protect the public being blown to pieces. What made it worse was that a woman who pledged to assist anyone in distress also lost her life. That was a hard one to see, and it is not something I want to relive. The only consolation is that there is a very special place reserved in the afterlife for heroes, and these three brave people would be immediately taken care of, no processing required.

Chapter Eight: 8:00 p.m.

"WE HAVE RECEIVED REPORTS FROM A SOURCE WHO DOES not wish to be identified that the reason SWAT entered the building is because the robbers were demanding large sums of money for each of the hostages. They had threatened to kill one person every fifteen minutes until they received the unspecified sum. We are now in the seventh hour of this negotiation, and that means that 105 casualties could be inside that bank right now. We have confirmed reports that there were injuries sustained by SWAT members and two fatalities. There was also a casualty among the firefighters that arrived at the scene. We are unable to identify them pending notification of the families. Channel 5 will continue to provide coverage of this event. Reporting live, Chip Rodgers, Channel 5 News."

The television was blasting this report at the clubhouse of the Commissioners of Chaos. The Commissioners of Chaos or "CommiChas" are a notoriously ruthless motorcycle club (MC). What made this club stand out from the others was that most of its members were descendants of other members. It was a true family environment, and usually titles would be passed down from father to son. The CommiChas rarely allowed someone to pledge the club from the outside. Those petitioning to join, or Prospects, went through immense scrutiny. It was generally thought by the club that family businesses stayed better off when they were family run. Also, it was much harder to infiltrate the club with informers that way. CommiChas figured that having a core membership that would live and die for the club was better than one that would grow by recruiting outsiders. Those who wanted to join an MC could have their pick of the numerous other clubs, the CommiChas thought. The Commissioners of Chaos was blood run.

Joe "Cheeky" Tanner had been paying close attention to the bank robbery all day. He wondered why he had not suggested it for his MC. He was the vice president of his chapter of a nationwide motorcycle gang. He had been a member of it since he was eighteen. His father had been a member before him and was one of the initial members to petition for a charter. He found a family among the men in his club, and it was the most important thing in the world to him. He had no family of his own to speak off, never having been married or having any kids. Although he did start to think about it with the cute nurse, Willow, whom he had started dating. He thought she could be a keeper and would make a good little house wifey when the time was right.

With his whole chapter robbing a bank, they could have been multimillionaires if they had only thought of it first. He kicked himself for not thinking of it. He returned his thoughts to the business at hand. The gang had been dealing with loss of turf in their sale of narcotics. In addition, their gunrunning business was getting harder and harder to run since they were running out of options on how to bring the firearms into the country. The city's port authority had increased security personnel at the port. Those guys had cracked down on the criminal activity therein. Joe's gang used to bring in firearms on shipping containers, but now that each container went through a scanner and metal detectors, his firearms were found rather quickly. The CommiChas had lost their entire shipment on the last run. There had been a big news story on it, seizure of arms worth upwards of $500,000 on the black market. It was covered by that reporter Chip Rodgers. It was the first time there was a report on his club. Up until then, no one had interfered with their business, and no law official could claim to have made a bust. It was well known that they were more than motorcycle enthusiasts, but it could not be proven that they were involved in any criminal activity until that bust. Drugs had become their best option to keep the club profitable.

Joe was designated to bring a pound of heroin to a rival gang member in hopes of a truce. It was a special blend made by one of their cooks. He hoped that they could become suppliers to their rivals and get a percentage of the profits. Joe's club could not afford to keep fighting over territory with other gangs encroaching on their city. There had been too much fighting on all sides, too many casualties, and everyone was losing out.

He secured the heroin in a compartment underneath his seat. Then Joe jumped on his custom Harley. He loved the roar of the engine and the vibration of his ride. He was most at peace when he was on his bike. He looked forward to the ride ahead, the opportunity to be at peace and just enjoy the road before conducting business.

Joe was headed for the rival gang's clubhouse on the other side of town. The destination was fairly secluded, just a country road near farm country. The clubhouse that belonged to the current rivals and perhaps future business partners blended in fairly well with the surrounding buildings. It was a converted barn. Big and red, he knew the first floor housed the den of the club as well as the bar. From what he heard, the sleeping quarters were on the second floor. As for where the club conducted its dirty business, that was in a shed out back. He knew all about the dirty business that went on in clubs. Violent interrogations, repackaging stolen merchandise, cutting drugs, and unloading guns all went on at his clubhouse.

As Joe was driving out of the city, he noticed that an eighteen-wheel rig was driving behind him, and it too made the turn off the highway onto the two-lane road. He immediately got suspicious of the truck and thought it may be someone after him and not just a good ol' trucking boy making a delivery. He sped up his Harley, and the truck sped up behind him. Okay, Joe thought, the truck was definitely after him. He knew that there would be a sharp curve about five miles ahead. There, the road he was on met a parallel road, and the two roads intersected into a T. Behind it there was a retaining wall. He knew he could speed ahead and make the curve no problem, and with any luck, the truck behind him would crash into that wall. So he rode along the country road doing eighty-five miles an hour, getting closer and closer to the other road that was coming up ahead. He finally made it, with the truck speeding behind him. Joe got ready to make the sharp turn when he saw that there was another eighteen wheeler in front of him already making a turn. *Crap* was the last thought that entered his head at 8:59 when he was crushed by the truck.

There was poor Joe by the side of the road, looking down at his pride and joy, his beautiful bike. And the bits of pink that used to be him. "Son of a bitch," he said. "That stupid truck did not see me." I made my way over to him but left a little bit of distance between us. I don't know what it is about bikers, but they freak me out even though they technically cannot do anything to me. I mean, what are they going to do? Kill me again? Yet there is something about them that makes me uneasy. I don't know if it is their attitude, the tough persona, or the fact that they can ride two wheels faster than should be possible and make it look easy. Damn, those guys sure are something. It is usually the bikers who accept their deaths the easiest. They never seem to wonder who I am. It's almost as if they expect me, and when I show up, they are pretty resigned to go.

As he was looking over his former self, I said to Joe, "Tough break there, Joe. Bet you did not see that one coming."

Without looking up, he said, "He did not see me coming. He collided right into me. Must be because it was getting dark."

"Or was it because he intended to hit you? Think about it. The vice president of CommiChas killed on the road. There is going to be a power vacuum, general disorder in your club. That is pretty good for the competition, don't you think?"

I saw him shake his head in disbelief and look up at me. "Not possible," he replied. I decided to change the subject.

"Hey, do you mind if we hang around here for a few minutes?

There is a hottie with a body coming by pretty soon. She's one of those real Hollywood types."

At this, he perked up and smiled and said, "Sure can. What is the plan?"

"Well, I will be escorting her to processing. It is really convenient that she is so close to here. Saves me a trip; this way I can take both of you to processing at the same time. It is where they determine what is next for you in the afterlife. As for you ..." I trailed off as I thought about what I was going to say.

He looked at me and broke into a grin and at the top of his lungs began to sing, "I'm on a highway to hell."

Catchy song, I thought. *Wonder who made it up*. I mulled on that while waiting for our girl to show up.

A little way down the road that Joe was just driving on, two trucks were driving. The two truck drivers got on their radios, and the guy who was following Joe said, "Thanks for coming, buddy. Got him there just in time for you to crush him."

The other driver replied, "No problem. The boss will be happy we eliminated the competition. See you back at the farm's clubhouse."

Chapter Nine: 9:00 p.m.

ELSIE WHITE WAS ONCE UPON A TIME NOT TOO LONG AGO seen as a golden child of the screen. She was adorable, covered in freckles, with reddish-blonde hair, dimples, and a megawatt smile. She could cry on cue and dance and sing, and for that the producers loved her. Her parents, unhappy with their marriage, pushed their daughter into show business and made an excellent profit off her. However, in her midtwenties, the roles were sparse for the actress, who had been pegged as a "hot mess." She showed up on set late and had a major attitude problem and a variety of addictions. Her publicist adamantly denied the allegations of addictions to the public. Meanwhile, she would give Sexaholics Anonymous, Alcoholic Anonymous, and other pamphlets to Elsie in private, saying, "Get some help, Elsie, before it is too late."

Elsie did not listen. She went to rehab, but only for the publicity. She went from the girl who hooked up with everyone to hooking up with one girl. The tabloids had a field day when she began the same-sex relationship. Then she became a reformed Christian preaching celibacy, and after that she went New Age and advocated becoming one with the earth and meditating. Through all of this change, her estate was dwindling.

She did not invest her money properly, and with the bad economy, the investments she did make took a nosedive. She could not make up that money with new roles; due to her crazy behavior, parts were harder to come by. Yet she managed to find a role that did look interesting to her. It was a part that showcased the lives of three bombshell beauties—Marilyn Monroe, Grace Kelly, and Brigitte Bardot. Their lives, loves, and losses.

Elsie was up for a part reenacting the early life of Grace Kelly. The casting agency in charge of the movie was not pleased with her being the frontrunner for the role, but it was no secret that she was sleeping with the producer of the film. So for now they had to deal with her. Elsie was a method actress. She loved to act exactly like her characters, so she had gone to Monaco. She enjoyed the city and talked to people about their deceased princess. Elsie even took to wearing a classic wardrobe to emulate the character. She was excited for the role! Whenever the press announced the contenders for leads in a movie, Elsie wanted to know what the buzz around the role was. So she Googled her name, Elsie White + Grace Kelly, to see what would come up. The first article that the search engine returned was not one she was expecting. It read: *A, B, C, D List ... See who is on it!*

Elsie had been on the A list for a few years in a row. Then, through no fault of her own, just a couple of drug charges and DUIs, she developed a reputation as a party child. And some snobby actresses started accusing her of being hard to work with and disruptive on the set. Those were ridiculous accusations in her mind.

She thought that being on the A list was maybe too much to hope for this year. Then again, "No publicity is bad publicity!" Checking for her name among the A list, she did not find it. She chalked it up to those darn rumors flying around. They must have caused some damage in the rankings. She scanned through the B list and then went through it again, sure of having missed her name. She did not find it on the second go either. She had a long sip of her vodka and water and tried scrolling again. There she wasn't!

She looked at the C list, and her name was not among the first people listed. In fact, she was there on the bottom with the tag line, "Elsie White on the C list but heading to D list fast. Only by the Grace of Kelly can save her."

What?

This could not be happening, she thought. Going to the D list, that was celebrity death. That was where people who won reality shows four years ago went. The D list stood for dead as far as Hollywood was concerned.

She had to win the part that she was up for. Now it had become a necessity. Well, any part was a necessity really, with the bills piling up and having to forgo things she really needed, like an assistant and getting her hair and makeup professionally done. Lately, the paparazzi was not really interested in her, so she did not have to look as glamorous, and plus, at $100 a makeup application and $150 for hair, she was having to cut it from the budget. *Ugh. Budget!* That had become a new word.

This Grace Kelly movie was the golden ticket, she thought. It would bring her back into the spotlight in a way that only a glamorous Hollywood icon turned princess can. She looked at herself in the mirror and said, "Channel her, channel her inner beauty and grace. Be Grace!"

She went into her closet and found her favorite vintage dress and put it on. Next she found a large pair of sunglasses, Chanel. She tucked them into her purse. She needed one final thing, a scarf. She took a pale blue silk scarf from the drawer. It was beautiful and so light that it almost felt like she was not wearing it. With that, she grabbed her keys from the hook on the wall and set out from her apartment. She was going for a drive. She always did her best thinking while driving. So she took her convertible out of the garage and decided to go for a ride out in the country. As she was driving down the two-lane road, she felt extremely free, and she decided to accelerate the car to feel the wind in her hair. The scarf she was wearing flapped behind her.

She got so distracted by the flapping scarf that she accelerated right into a truck that was completing a turn after killing Joe Tanner. She went into it headfirst. Elsie White died at 9:00 p.m. on the dot.

Joe was initially more concerned about his bike than his own demise. Outlaws—they always meet their death the most calmly. It is like they know they are destined for it and that today was the day, so they just accept it. Little miss movie star was not as calm. She started freaking out!

"What do you mean I am dead? I am supposed to start shooting a movie! I am going to be Grace Kelly!"

"Well, maybe you can see if you can meet her. She enjoys meeting her fans. I am sorry, but I am supposed to help you leave earth now. Come on."

"But she was killed because she was strangled by her scarf in the car, right?"

"No, she died of a stroke at the age of fifty-three when she lost control of her car and was involved in a collision. The scarf story is just a common misconception. But she died in a car, and you died in a car, so way to take the role seriously. You really committed to it!"

That seemed to satisfy her, and she turned her attention to Joe, who was admiring the starlet. Both Joe and Elsie realized that they had died in a car accident a minute apart, which made them feel like they had a bond. The fact that both had been killed by the same truck only deepened that bond. I guess they felt like they had to have some substance to their meeting because they started flirting right away. I mean in a hands-on, touchy-feely flirting kind of way. I managed to get them to the processing center still lip locked.

"Chip Rodgers here. I have been covering this event all day, but just now I have been given an exclusive interview with the man who orchestrated this entire robbery. He is joining us via webcam. Sir, we are broadcasting your interview to the entire city. Is there something you would like to say to the viewers out there watching this program?"

"Yes. First of all, I am sorry that members of the SWAT team got injured. Their deaths were without cause. Make no mistake; the men here are all sorry to hear that they have perished. There was no need for that. This could have all been resolved by now, and there is no need for people to get hurt. We are making a simple cash demand, and we intend on releasing all of the employees as soon as that demand is met. No other lives have to be lost. This bank is covered by a multi-billion-dollar insurance corporation, and they will suffer no cash loses. It is simple; they have the power to resolve this issue without anyone else getting hurt. It is in their hands to end this crisis; no other lives have to be lost. As a show of good faith to a peaceful resolution, my men will release two hundred hostages this hour under the condition that all of the SWAT members evacuate with them as well."

Chapter Ten: 10:00 p.m.

BY NOW, CHIP HAD GOTTEN WEARY. THE EXHAUSTION HAD begun to set in. Nine hours of continuous reporting was getting to be too much. He had been covering the crisis all day, and the excitement that had gotten him through the first few hours had begun to wane. Now he just wanted it to be over one way or another. He wanted to drink a scotch and go to bed. The station had other plans for him. It was ten o'clock, time for the regularly scheduled news program. Here they could recap the day's events. The station had already compiled a reel of the most exciting and tense moments at the standoff. They were intending to air it and have Chip comment on the situation. News was the lifeblood of the station, for the ten o'clock viewers eagerly tuned in before heading to bed. This was Channel 5's most profitable program. This would be the last of the updates that most viewers would watch until they heard the resolution on their morning news or while reading their morning papers on their tablets. The station manager kept shouting at Chip through his earphone to give him more drama. Chip was too tired to comply.

Instead, he stated, "It is ten o'clock here at the scene of the Credit Bank hostage crisis. The negotiator Sergeant Stevens is arranging to release more hostages from the building. More updates as they become available. Chip Rodgers here. Back to the studio for other news."

Lacey Lowe was once an exotic dancer. When she had a son, she decided that she could no longer do her line of work. So she became a bartender at the club where she used to work as a dancer. It made her feel a bit better to be serving drinks instead of serving lap dances. She knew it was not the ideal job, and most of the time she felt like a cliché, a single mom working at a strip club. She thought about getting other jobs, but she knew that even people with advanced degrees were having a hard time finding work, so she would not fare much better with a junior-college education. She resolved to work at the club until times got a little better and until she could find a better career.

While working at the club, she met a lawyer named Duncan. At first, she did not pay him much attention. He was just like every other suit claiming to be there for the happy hour and the steak. She was polite enough to him but never friendly. It was not until one fateful day that she went to cash a check from her ex for child support that things changed. She needed the check to clear in order to pay the rent that month. When it bounced, the humiliation and despair were too much to bear. She ended up breaking down in tears at the tellers till she slid down and let the tears fall as she sat on the floor. Duncan was one queue over in the business banking line when he saw her. The other patrons of the bank pretended to not see her in hysterics but were in reality overanalyzing the drama queen and feeling embarrassed for her. Duncan stepped in to help her. He walked over to Lacey in his crisp gray suit and laid a soft, warm hand on her shoulder. He knelt down, and with real concern in his voice, he asked, "Is there something I can do? Would you like me to help you up, and we can talk about what is troubling you?"

Through tearstained eyes, Lacey recognized him from the club but gave him no indication that she knew who he was. True to his word, he walked her over to a coffee shop next to the bank and asked what the matter was. She told him that the check for child support had bounced and she needed it to help cover the rent. She proceeded to tell Duncan how her ex always let her down. How she was having a hard time raising her son, and even though she loved him, she wondered how she could support them both. Duncan listened patiently, and when she was finished, he asked what the amount of the check was. When she replied that it was five hundred, he calmly went into his wallet and pulled out five freshly printed one-hundred-dollar bills and gave them to her. She was stunned.

Lacey was torn between accepting charity and promising to pay it back. She wondered what she would have to do to repay him for it. When she asked him, he simply replied, "I know what it is like to go through a hard time and need assistance. There will come a time when you are well off and can get anything you desire on your own. When you are down on your luck and no one is willing to help, it is the person who does offer you assistance who you will remember most. All I ask is you remember me fondly in the future."

Over the next few visits to her club, Lacey was much friendlier to Duncan. She wondered if there was more to this man. He stayed friendly enough and never overstepped his boundaries. Lacey ended up developing a bit of a crush on him and was the one who asked him out. Quickly, a romance blossomed. He was a little older but definitely rich, and he promised to take care of her and her son. He had delivered on that promise and let them live in a condo downtown.

About an hour ago, she had received a phone call from Duncan's wife that went something like this: "Listen, you little tramp, I knew all about your affair with my husband, but I figured if you were giving it up to him, he would not come around wanting to have sex with me. So I let it slide. But now that he is dead, I do not want you living in a condo that now belongs to me. My daughters will get the condo instead. You have until midnight to evacuate whatever belongings you have in there, or security is coming to throw you out on your cheap ass!" With that, she hung up.

Lacey was shocked. In the span of a minute, she found out that she had lost her lover and her home. She was a bit clouded in her thinking because she had started drinking the bottle of wine that she had prepared for her and Duncan around 5:00 p.m. When he had not shown up by seven, she cracked open another bottle from his reserve selection. She was mad because she thought he was standing her up. A third bottle was just opened a few minutes ago. Lacey thought it would be a good way to get herself to sleep, as she was too upset at being stood up by Duncan. But then she got the phone call and found out that he had died. Her poor Duncan! And now she had only a few hours to collect her belongings, her son, and figure out a place to live. She could not do that while she was groggy. She decided to take a few aspirins to try to clear her head, and then she realized it would take awhile for that to work. She thought maybe a swim might do the trick. Plus, this would be the last time she would be able to swim in the pool of the luxury condominium development. She might as well enjoy it! As for packing, it was not like she owned very much that she could take from the condo. The furniture was all Duncan's. At best, she could take her clothes and a few pieces of jewelry. Duncan had not exactly showered her with jewels that she could pawn off now for some quick cash.

So she changed into a bathing suit and made her way downstairs to the pool. She tried doing a few laps but found it exhausting. So she decided to just take a minute and relax in the hot tub. In there, she closed her eyes for just a minute. When she awoke, she saw a man standing over her.

"Can I help you?" she asked.

"No, I am here to help you, ma'am," the tall, handsome stranger replied.

"With the evacuation from this building?"

"Well, no, with the evacuation from life. You drowned just now, ma'am. I am sorry to break the news to you, but now you need to come with me. I am going to take you to a place, and they will arrange for your afterlife."

At that, Lacey broke down and started screaming and sobbing. She could not be dead. She could not be having the worst day of her life and then just have it end because she was careless. She had a little boy upstairs asleep in his bed who had no idea what had happened to his mommy. She was inconsolable, and I could not take her with me, not in that state. A person has to accept death before he or she can come with me. Otherwise the person stays in limbo. She was falling on her knees crying, and I knew we would not be able to make progress with her like that. I told her that she could take some time to cry and compose herself, and I would be back to get her. I was just going to the children's hospital ward down the street. I would be back in an hour or so.

I figured she would not do much harm in one hour while she cried. I would be able to take her back with another person.

I had to figure out who the people from Karl's list were. So far, only the people from my list had perished. I had not gotten the envelope with the list of casualties from him, and it looked like the crisis would be resolved one way or another very soon.

Chapter Eleven: 11:00 p.m.

"CHIP RODGERS REPORTING HERE AT THE SCENE OF CREDIT Bank. The intense standoff between the Credit Bank robbers and the police is still going on. In case you have just joined us, the hostage crisis began at 1:00 p.m. this afternoon, and throughout it, more than half the hostages have been released. This triumph has also been coupled with tragedy as two SWAT members, Luke Warkowski and Steve Brown, died in an explosion inside the building, as well as Nancy Grace, a member of the fire department who was killed while attempting to rescue Brown. Now the head of the robbery team has agreed to free all of the remaining hostages in exchange for Sergeant Stevens talking to the orchestrator in a face-to-face meeting."

Now I was fuming. It was eleven o'clock in the evening, and this whole hostage situation was likely to be resolved soon. The majority of the hostages were released. There was no large-scale blowup. At the start of the situation, there were over a thousand people in that building, and now all of them were getting released. So no disaster was likely to happen. It was time to go pay Karl a visit.

I found him taking a load off at his desk, with a bottle of brandy in hand, buzzed to the nines.

"Karl, what the hell? You said this was going to be a major disaster. So far, there has been no disaster! What kind of game are you running here?"

"Gotta level with you, bud. It was never going to be a major disaster. I pawned this job off on you so that it wouldn't affect my statistics. They can't move me if my numbers are fantastic! Fact is I am getting demoted."

"They are demoting you? What for?"

"Oh, apparently there have been some complaints from the staff. They say I am rude, rush them through the process, take too much pleasure in my morbid work. Etc etc. etc. You know, they are just whiney, and they think I am a jerk because I tell them to hurry it up, suck it up, and deal with it. To top it all off, the higher-ups accuse me of stealing ideas for my own profit."

He took a swig from his bottle and shook his head.

"Now they are demoting me to working with the nouveaubodies. I hate dealing with the NBs. That is why I got out of Daily Deaths in the first place. They are so unstable and miserable!"

"Well, they did just die, and it is one of life's greatest shocks. You don't expect them to be completely cooperative. You have to be able to make it a little bit easier for them—show up how they want you to show up, explain what will happen, and make them feel better about it," I suggested.

He took another swig.

"Yeah, that is not my deal. I am how I am, and I like the big jobs with lots of carnage and the big, cushy office. And they can deal with it, and why don't you go deal with your bleeding hearts one-on-one cases. Trust me; someone is going to bite it at that bank. Don't let the door hit you on the way out."

I walked out of Karl's office knowing I was right about the guy all along. He was a corporate kiss-ass who was two-faced and willing to stab anyone in the back to stay on top. I looked at my schedule. Lacey had died, and I told her that I would be back for her. I had most of this hour free, and it was my last hour. It meant that I had to go back and get Kevin.

You thought I would regret bending the rules, right? Thought that Kevin would have spilled his little guts and told people about me. That he maybe even drew a picture of me and showed it to everyone he knew?

Well, people can surprise you, and even after meeting as many as I have, I managed to be surprised by little Kevin Johnson.

When I arrived at his hospital room, he was peacefully asleep in his bed. When I woke him and told him it was time to go, he gave a cheerful smile and said, "Okay. Ready, Freddie!"

I was curious and asked, "How can you be so cheerful?"

"Well, I was sick for most of my life. I never really had a chance to be a kid. I had a great family, and I loved them, and I know they love me. I know I will see them again someday, but for now I get to see my grandpa and be a kid in heaven, playing with toys, eating all the candy I want, and having no bedtime!"

I never mentioned anything about no bedtime, but it was fairly accurate. Rules were pretty lax where he was going. But I also had to remark on something.

"Kevin, you surprised me. You did not say anything about seeing me today or that it was going to be your last day here. Why was that?"

He had a thoughtful look on his face, and he took a minute before he answered.

"Most of the time when people look at me, they see a poor, little sick kid; they don't see Kevin. Merry knows me. She played trains with me, and we camped inside because I couldn't really go outside. Mom and Dad, well, they are Mom and Dad. They worry, but I had a chance to tell them I loved them. I wanted them to remember me as me. There was no need to make them feel bad about it being my last day alive."

I thought about that and was pretty impressed. There was a reason we were not able to grant second chances to people; it was because they could reveal the mystery of what came in the afterlife. A few of them had done just that. They went to the media and talked about their near-death experience, the white lights feeling of peace, etc. It really bothered the executives of Deaco that they went and did that. The reason they did not describe the reaper is because we cannot really reveal ourselves until we are sure that there is no coming back to life.

Some see a hazy image of us and just assume we are the people they want to greet them. It is because they see what they want to see. Once they accept death, they see me for who I really am.

Kevin had given me his word, and he kept it. I was impressed because a seven-year-old had done something that people three times his age could not do. Heck, people even ten times his age could not be trusted. Seventy-year-olds tend to be the chattiest. I was impressed by this kid and his great attitude.

He looked over my shoulder and asked, "Why is the pretty lady crying?" I turned to see what he was looking at and saw Lacey. I had been so distracted by Kevin I had not even noticed her. Had she decided to follow me back? Lacey was still crying because of her accidental overdose. I meant to go over and give her a talking to; she was supposed to stay where I left her. But before I had a chance to get to her, Kevin walked up to her and asked, "Why are you so sad, lady?"

She looked at him for the first time and said, "I am sad because I made a big mistake, and because of that, my son lost his mommy."

He looked at her thoughtfully and said, "Well, I am a little boy who does not have a mommy anymore. Maybe you could pretend to be my mom, and I could pretend to be your son for a little while, until our real families meet us in heaven." With that, she stopped sobbing, nodded, and gave him a hug.

Seeing that really tugged on the old heartstrings. Man, this kid could make even the biggest cynic a believer in human goodness. He really was something. I could see both were ready to take the next step into the afterlife.

Occasionally, two nouveaubodies connect in the afterlife. They bond over something. Sometimes it can be complete strangers like Kevin and Lacey who fill roles for each other in death that they had in life. He the role of a son, she the role of a mother. At other times, people can find their soul mate when they are least looking—in this case, once they died in a car accident, like Joe and Elsie. Others look forward to connecting with a person who has passed away before them, like Mrs. Wong, who looked forward to seeing her husband.

I have decided to reveal the last twelve stories of the last twelve people I encountered at their moment of passing. Now it is time to tell of the last one, Karl's case. It was the single name written on the piece of paper in the envelope he gave me.

Chapter Twelve: 12:00 a.m. Midnight

Tom Sutton had worked in a manufacturing company for twenty years. They had produced circuit boards for computers. He got the job as a young engineer in the late seventies. This was when computers were honking massive objects that only large corporations and governments made use of. In his time at the firm, he saw computers get smaller and smaller and faster and faster. Computers became capable of doing ever greater things. Over time, he also saw the profit margins decrease for the company in their North American facilities. He dreaded the concept of globalization. For him, that translated to outsourcing, the loss of his job to someone overseas who would make a fraction of his hourly salary in a day. The company held out long enough, but last year they shut down the production facility.

Sutton had been in charge of thirty people. With the loss of their jobs and the bad global economy, many employees had not been able to bounce back. Tom was one of the lucky ones. He got a job as an IT technician at Credit Bank, but he knew the stories of his former employees. He checked out their lives on Facebook, and many lives were grim. There were losses of homes, broken marriages, etc. Lives changed by the lack of income. He felt personally responsible for every person on that floor, and he wanted each of them to bounce back and have a life again. While working on the computers at Credit Bank, he noticed how the monetary transactions were made. He also noticed the profits that were made despite the economy. The millions of dollars the company made every day. Millions that went back into the executives' pockets. He hated that the workingman was not able to get some of that money. He thought about what his employees could do with a couple of million. Retire in comfort. Send their kids to school. Buy a sailboat and cruise around the world with the missus. His thoughts got more and more elaborate. Tom imagined telling Jimmy, one of the eldest displaced employees and one who had not found a new job, that he could send his kid to that fancy university in California and that tuition was completely covered. Every day, the thoughts got more and more concrete and realistic. Soon he had a plan for each of his employees. He imagined the look on their faces when he would tell them that they were millionaires. After a few months, the fantasies were no longer good enough. He wanted them to become reality.

Tom wanted to change everyone's life, to give them lots of money so they would never have to worry again. At first, he floated the idea by his closest friends, Jimmy and Mark, at his Memorial Day barbeque. He explained how it could be done, and to his surprise, they were interested in doing it, if not for themselves then for their families. They had mouths to feed, things they wanted to do. Slowly they began developing the plan step by step. Carefully they began to recruit some of the former staff members. By August, the plan was ready to be put into action. The plan was simple and genius in its execution. Tom thought that rather than rob one bank branch, he would hold up the corporation itself and demand millions, enough for each of the robbers. He would ask for an exorbitant amount, knowing the bank would not pay it. But they would pay part of it, enough for all the men to live comfortably for the rest of their lives.

He printed out keycards with fake identities on the company's own computer system. He allowed the keycards to have full access to the floors and the vault at the branch. Then on the day of the robbery, he had two robbers go to each of the corporation's floors (the first floor was the bank branch), and three men were later stationed in the branch itself. It was very simple. The two men went up to each of the floors strapped with explosive devices that were duds. They were never going to explode, but the employees did not know that. Also, each of them carried an AK 47 assault rifle, "borrowed" from a military barrack that

Tom's nephew worked at. From the control room, the phones were disabled so that no one could make a call from his or her desk. It was standard procedure at Credit Bank that all employees turn in their cell phones at the beginning of the day in order to ensure no security breaches. These could have included employees taking pictures of high net worth accounts, in order to get account numbers, or texting numbers to an outside source, etc. Next part of the plan was an e-mail sent en masse to each of the employees. In the e-mail, there was a video attached. Once opened, the masked men were shown on screen. The men stated: "We have occupied your building. If our demands are not met, one employee from each floor will be murdered every fifteen minutes. To show we are not kidding, here is how it will be done."

Then on the screen Darren from the mailroom was shown. Everyone knew Darren; he came to each of the floors delivering mail. His sandy blond hair was in disarray, his bright blue eyes bloodshot and rimmed with tears. He had been crying and was obviously petrified. The next image shown was a big blade on the screen, and it only took a few seconds for it to slice Darren's throat. Darren's body crumpled. Then the masked men returned, stating, "Don't panic. No one else has to be made example of! We just want the money. If your bosses don't give it to us, then you could be next."

This of course caused mass panic, and that is when the masked men made their entrance waving their weaponry.

Now Darren was not actually hurt. He was part of the plan. Darren had a day job in the mailroom, but really he wanted to be an actor and get the hell out of the corporate world as soon as he made enough money to spend all his time in LA auditioning. So when he was approached with a figure of $250,000 to give the performance of a lifetime, he jumped at the chance and brought his own props, a giant realistic blade made out of plastic, fake blood, and a strong pair of acting chops. He was done with his role in a few minutes. The rest of his job would be to lie on the floor for any people who would be brought into the mailroom as hostages. He was to lie in the middle of the floor in a pool of fake blood as a reminder of what could happen to the hostages if they did not cooperate. The robbers counted on none of the hostages approaching Darren while they were in the room. They would be too scared and shell-shocked by their own trauma to approach their fallen coworker.

The masked robbers keeping them in the mailroom would prevent anyone from getting too close. The plan was to not hurt anyone, but one person was removed from each floor every fifteen minutes and held in the large mailroom that was under the building and free of any windows and extremely soundproof. Thus the illusion to the coworkers was complete. One poor soul was dragged away by masked gunmen, and all others presumed he or she would not return. Soon the panic was so great that all the employees turned to the bosses and demanded that they give in to the demands.

"Give them the money, give them anything they want!" the employees pleaded.

The compromise from Tom's side was releasing a floor for every three transactions made. Each transaction was valued at ten million dollars, sent to an untraceable account in the Caymans. Once three of the members had their sum, the floor was released, and robbers would be left behind just to monitor the situation and assist the other robbers with whatever was needed. This meant extra manpower on all the exits, some extras in the mailroom for crowd control, and extra muscle on the top floor where all the high-paid executives had their offices. By the end of the night, that was the only floor left full of people. At this point in time, forty-five people, including Darren, the first victim, were presumed dead by the authorities. There were three actual casualties. The SWAT officers and the firefighter. Tom was sorry they died, but he needed his plan to go off perfectly, and that meant no one could take them down prior to completion. Fifty of the top-ranking employees and executives were at the top floor of the building.

Tom had evacuated the rest of the floors. Among the released hostages were the gunmen who blended in with the crowd. The gunmen stripped off their masks and discarded their weapons. They changed clothes into casual Friday wear and blended in with the people who were so scared and so relieved to be getting out that they did not pay attention to the few unfamiliar faces that were leaving the building with them. With the crowd gathered outside and persons leaving the building, the authorities were too overwhelmed to check every person. So the robbers blended in and got away.

For the most part, the hard work was behind them. The only gunmen left were Jimmy and Mark on the top floor. After the events of the day, two were enough for the scared-stiff executives who had no idea what was going on in the building or how many people had been let go. They did the math and assumed at least forty-five were dead and that any one of them could be next. The COO (chief operating officer) was one of the first victims taken in hour one. This scared the rest of the top executive team. When the gunmen told them that the executives were the last ones left in the building and would be killed unless they complied with the demands, the executives decided that it was time to comply. Their lives were too valuable not to comply. At the end of the night, down in the mailroom with the forty-plus hostages, one of Tom's masked men said, "Get this body out of here. It is starting to stink!" Darren was dragged away, leaving a pool of blood through the door. Once out the doors, he got up on his feet and took the duffle bag containing $250,000 and a wig and change of clothes. He got out of the building no problem.

The man in charge of handling the situation was the Senior Negotiator Sergeant Tony Stevens. He was a career police officer, having joined right after his stint in the army. On the job for twenty-five years, it was all he wanted to do. He had been married before, but that had fallen apart many years ago. He had no children. Police work had become the most important thing to him. He loved it. His calm demeanor and quick thinking got him promoted to head negotiator for the city. He was confident that there would be a solution with the man who held the bank hostage. When he entered the building, the elevator was functioning. He was instructed to come to a certain floor and meet with the man he viewed as a terrorist.

Sergeant Stevens walked into the darkened building where only emergency lights were on. He found the leader of the robbers (or terrorists, in his eyes) sitting calmly in a chair waiting for him with a gun in his hand. Stevens said to him, "Well, I guess this is it! You plan on walking out of here? You killed a lot of people! Yeah, you let some go, but I don't think it will go very well for you out there. There is a special place in hell reserved for men like you. But first I will want to watch you fry in the electric chair. You'll never be free again."

"True," the masked man said. "I do not think I will ever be free in this country, so perhaps I will let you take care of me, finish me off with a bullet. But maybe before I go, you want to see who has been causing you all this grief?" With that, he slowly peeled off his mask and said, "Well, I guess now you have to shoot me!" And with that, Sergeant Stevens raised his gun. A shot echoed through the space, and it was deafening in the eerie silence.

"Chip Rodgers here reporting at the Credit Bank where an intense standoff has been taking place all day. It looks like the head negotiator Sergeant Stevens has just come out triumphantly. He is waving a white flag and going into the crowd … Sergeant Stevens, a comment?"

Stevens turned to Chip and walked up to the reporter holding the microphone.

"Today was a difficult day for all the employees at Credit Bank. I wish to personally thank the men and women who assisted in this crisis. I extend my deepest condolences to all the families who have lost loved ones today. Especially to officers Kozlowski and Brown and Firefighter Grace—they paid the ultimate sacrifice for the freedom of many. I wish to assure the public that the situation is now under control. The men responsible have been captured. The leader of this operation was killed when he pulled a gun on me."

With that, Stevens thanked Chip and walked off the camera.

By the time SWAT entered the building and found each of the floors empty, the last robbers were gone. They had left through a service entrance that no one was paying attention to in the last mass exodus of hostages. The building had been deemed clear by the triumphant negotiator Sergeant Stevens, and he calmly went to the police station and spoke to the captain, where he was congratulated on doing an amazing job and freeing the hostages. He thanked the captain for the commendation and stated that he would be ending his career. He stated that he would like to give his resignation effective immediately. The captain regretfully accepted the resignation and let Sergeant Stevens walk out the door. After SWAT had done a complete sweep through the building, they went to the gruesome task of retrieving the perished hostages in the mailroom. They were surprised to find forty-four people alive and terrified, looking at them with immense gratitude in their eyes. Where they expected to find the body of Darren, they instead found a man with an army tattoo on his forearm that looked incredibly like that of Sergeant Stevens, the negotiator.

Tom Sutton had walked out of the police station into a waiting car and was then taken to a private jet. He had no problems getting onto the plane as Sergeant Stevens, off on a vacation. Of course he would not have a problem because he looked identical to Stevens. That was the good thing about being a twin.

The two brothers were split up following their parents' nasty divorce. Tony Sutton took on the name Stevens after his stepdad when his mom remarried. The brothers hadn't spoken in over thirty years, but remarkably, they had aged much the same. Ironically, Tom did not have a lot of guilt about pulling the trigger on his brother. He was killed in the line of duty, so the insurance company would pay a high premium that would go to his family. A premium Tom knew Tony had. Just like he knew that Tony had tried to take his life a few times before, so really, he had just done him a favor. Tom Sutton felt no guilt as the plane took off for the Caymans.

Tony, on the other hand, was very pissed off. "He just killed me. My own brother just killed me. He let everyone else go and just killed me to get away with it! How do I get him back? Huh? How do I get justice?" he asked me.

"Sorry, Tony, I am just a delivery guy. You might need to take this issue up with processing."